Bad Latitude – A Jack Rackham Adventure

David Ebright

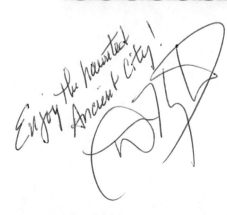

Enjoy the haunted Ancient city!

Booklocker.com, Inc.
2008

Many Thanks......

Nothing worthwhile is ever accomplished alone and I want to acknowledge those that offered encouragement, advice, and suggestions along the way. Special hugs for my kids, Michael, Christopher and Christine. Thanks also to Valerie, Lee, my friends at DBK, and Matt K.

Y'all are the best.

For my dad – who taught me to dream

For my mom – whose hard work gave me the tools to chase my dreams

For my grandkids – Jack and Isabel – Always Have Happy Dreams!

AND

For my loving wife Deb – You must be a dream - So don't wake me. LYD!

BAD LATITUDE
A JACK RACKHAM ADVENTURE

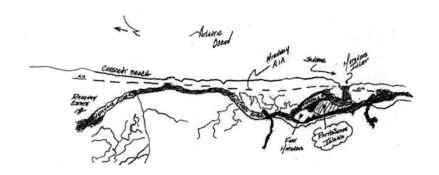

Prologue

24 September 1696

There was no escaping the hurricane's fury. Disaster struck when the center mast snapped, toppling with a thunderous crash as the doomed ship listed hard to port, exposing its massive keel. The hull's planking splintered inward from the pounding of the raging seas, flooding the cargo holds, forcing the crew and passengers to scramble from the shelter below into the teeth of the violent storm. Solomon Cresson, a stout member of the crew, was the last to climb the twisting ladder to the deck above. With the Captain of the ship missing and presumed lost, Cresson took charge. He shouted above the gale, ordering all aboard to stay with the ship for as long as there was a structure to grasp. The listing vessel was aground in the shallows, beam to sea, being smashed by fierce waves and buffeted by driving winds as the passengers clung to the fallen

David Ebright

rigging, struggling for survival against the rushing flood, and collapsing timbers.

By first light, it was over. Those not drowned or washed to sea were greeted with the spectacular view of a white sandy beach, two hundred yards from their wrecked merchant ship, *The Reformation*. Twelve souls had been lost. The survivors, battered, bloodied, and exhausted, salvaged what they could from the ship. A single long boat, lashed to the bow, was all that remained of the original four, the last hope to cheat death once more. The crew heaved it overboard and shuttled passengers, bodies and a meager supply of provisions ashore. Cresson made the last trip alone, carefully concealing a wooden crate containing a fortune in gold and gemstones, the property of the shipping company. He had planned the theft long before the ship left port.

Rowing toward shore, with thirty yards of surf to conquer, he stared in horror as a band of Jobe tribesman rushed upon the stranded castaways. As the small boat scraped the sandy bottom, Cresson tossed the box carelessly into the shallows and charged into the center of the skirmish. Knowing they were in Spanish territory, he roared at the attackers, mixing fluent Spanish with intimidating gestures. The ruse worked and the Jobes abandoned the survivors to return to their village. With the reprieve, the crew and passengers prepared for the long night ahead while Cresson secretly retrieved the treasure from the sea. Hidden from the others, he buried the gold behind a dune, which aligned with the broken masthead of the listing ship.

As darkness fell, the warriors, led by their *Cacique*, returned. Unable to resist, the outnumbered survivors were herded to the tribal village, stripped of all possessions, and held captive. Killing the stranded travelers was not an option for the

Indian King, as the Spaniards controlling the area would view such a slaughter as an act of aggression.

For weeks the group was routinely beaten, degraded, and deprived of necessities by their captors. Despite being a prime target of the cruel treatment, Solomon continued his attempts at intimidation, using demanding tones, and threatening antics. Seeing the swaggering Cresson as a potential danger, the King ordered him to leave the group and proceed northward to St. Augustine, where the largest Spanish colony had been established. The remaining captives would be released an agonizing week later. This decree played into Cresson's hands, allowing him to collect the gold before starting his journey toward the massive fortress, *Castillo de San Marcos.*

Following torturous weeks of lonely perseverance, Cresson, feverish with infection, and suffering with painfully blistered flesh, finally caught his first glimpse of the Spanish settlement. Emaciated, and pathetically weak, he confronted a new dilemma, realizing that the Spaniards would steal his fortune upon arrival. Pain, hunger, and exposure would be endured for yet another night while he devised a plan to protect the treasure he had labored to carry.

Choosing an area of heavy brush, at the edge of a clearing where three rivers converged, two miles south of the outpost, Cresson made camp. Fear of discovery overwhelmed his need for the warming benefit of a fire. The sacrifice of comfort ultimately saved his life.

Beneath an orange colored midnight moon, nearly one hundred natives from the Timacua tribe assembled at the river's edge and marched to within yards of Cresson's hideout. He was startled from his restless sleep by their approach. Quickly and silently, he crawled deeper into the snake-infested thicket, desperately stifling his panicked gasps for breath with one callused hand. From his new vantage point, he could see that the natives were giants, all standing at or near seven feet tall. His pulse quickened and his body trembled, certain that death was imminent when he realized that the fortune he had hefted for so many miles lay partially exposed at the edge of the clearing. Its discovery would surely bring about his end.

Cresson watched as a secret tribal ritual unfolded. Hoisted upon a litter of palm fronds and pine branches was the body of a leader of great importance. With menacing chants, five holes were dug, one in the center of the clearing, and four just beyond. While the fierce looking warriors surrounded the center gravesite, the corpse was gently and reverently lowered into the pit and arranged as if seated. The four given the privilege of carrying the body, silently completed the honorary duty of filling the grave. Cresson could never have anticipated what followed.

The pallbearers, showing no trace of fear or sadness, climbed into the four remaining burial pits, assumed sitting positions, and calmly folded their arms. Once properly situated, the tribal elders proceeded to bury the men alive as the rhythmic chants changed to sorrowful high-pitched wails. Two hours following the start of the eerie ceremony, the Timucuans marched off in a somber procession to waiting canoes and paddled south through the darkness.

Solomon Cresson, using only his bare hands, buried his stolen prize in the freshly dug soils of the gravesite, at the feet of the noble warrior, silently vowing to return one day to retrieve it.

More than three hundred years later..........

1

Southbound Yankee

Jack Rackham spent summers with his grandparents in the ancient haunted city of St Augustine Florida. Through the years, his grandfather shared with him endless stories and legends of pirates, ghosts, and long lost riches. Learning everything possible about treasure hunting was their primary hobby, spending visits together trying to outdo one other with their knowledge and collection of tales and related oddities. Jack thought Pop cheated, by making up wild yarns that couldn't be traced to history. He never minded. Pop's tales were always outrageously entertaining.

Pirates and lost treasure were a part of the family's heritage and had motivated Pop to work through a maze of difficult clues, leading him to his first discovery of a fortune in gold coins and artifacts. The resulting wealth made it possible for Pop to retire and pursue his love of treasure hunting and storytelling full time. Jack benefited from Pop's good luck, sharing the pleasures of sun, sand, and surf while investigating stories and mysteries that he hoped would someday lead to his own successful search for gold. At the age of nearly sixteen, he had found his passion.

It was the night of June 14th and Jack was flying the red-eye to Jacksonville Florida. His flight would not arrive at JIA until one-thirty-five in the morning. It was late for his grandparents to have to pick him up, but he knew they wouldn't mind. Chances were he and Pop would sit up until dawn trading outlandish stories anyway.

"Please fasten your seatbelts as we prepare to land." The long awaited message came over the intercom. "We will be on the ground within ten minutes."

Jack rummaged through his carry-on and found a black doo rag and eye patch. He would greet his grandparents in style. There was no doubt they would laugh, they laughed all the time. After touchdown, he tied the bandanna in place and slipped on the patch. They went well with the heavy gold hoop in his ear, but he wished he had more than just the light blonde stubble on his chin to make his appearance more authentic. It would be the start of the non-stop teasing that would go on for the next ten weeks. He couldn't hold back the smile as he exited to the concourse.

"Well, if it ain't Cap'n Kidd," said Pop. "Maybe next time you could pick a later flight."

Nan squeezed her way past to reach her grandson. "At least let him get to the house before you start your nonsense. Jack, you can't possibly get any bigger or better looking."

It was true. He was a good-looking kid with bright blue eyes, a perfect smile, and thick blonde hair touching the top of his shoulders. Standing tall at six feet two inches, he had broad shoulders and a well-defined upper body that tapered to a thin waist. It was common for girls to stare and smile.

"Hi Nan. You too old-timer. I half expected to see you with a peg leg by now."

They hugged tightly before marching off toward the baggage claim. As the doo rag and eye patch were tucked into the carry-on, Pop asked if maybe the earring should join the rest of the costume, earning Pop a quick poke to the ribs and a wink from Nan as he mumbled the suggestion.

"Next year you'll have your license and I plan on leavin' a car at the airport so you can drive yourself. I'm gettin' too old to be keepin' up with your crazy flight arrangements," announced Pop. "A man doesn't stay this good lookin' for this long without plenty of shut eye." Pop never passed on the opportunity to offer an exaggerated opinion of himself to his grandson.

The man was in remarkably good shape for his age. Favoring cargo shorts, tee shirts and flip-flops, he carried a deep year-round tan to go with his craggy features, while the ever-present baseball cap, with logos describing tropical locations, helped hide his thinning hair. Pop's goatee, now pure white, combined with a pair of intense aqua blue eyes, made him appear intimidating despite being a shade less than six feet tall.

Jack laughed at the thought of either of his grandparents admitting to getting old but played along. "No problem you ole geezer, but I want to know ahead of time what kind of car you plan on leaving for me. A new red Jeep would work."

"After that geezer crack you can bet it'll be somethin' real nice, maybe a Ford Pinto with faded paint and mismatched hubcaps. Geezer indeed. I can still run circles around you, and don't you be forgettin' it." Pop was trying not to grin as he worked to gain the advantage. Jack wasn't fooled by the bark. The smile never left Pop's eyes.

The ride from the airport took less than an hour. Pop had set the cruise control at eighty-five and they were running with the truckers. "We drive faster down here than the dad gum Yanks from up your way."

As they passed through the gates to the estate, Jack noticed that all of the lights were burning throughout the house. Pop complained that he didn't own the electric company but Nan would never leave her home looking dark. It had to appear warm and inviting for her grandson's arrival. While pulling the Escalade into the garage, Pop groused, to no one in particular, about the bugs splattered on the grill and windshield. He was meticulous about the care of his vehicles.

Nan dismissed the grumbling. "Don't worry; you'll have it cleaned before anyone is awake tomorrow."

"That's beside the point. Why I let you talk me into buyin' a black vehicle, I'll never know," complained Pop. "Nothin' but work. You just can't keep the blasted thing clean."

As they entered the kitchen, the coffee pot started to brew as if on cue. "Looks like I misjudged the trip by a few minutes. I was wantin' a fresh cup of high test waitin' for me when I hit the door. Well, I suspect, my dear Jackson that you've managed to make up some tall tales chock full of the usual blarney and I'll have to listen and pretend to believe 'em." Pop always used Jack's real name when getting down to business.

"Blarney my eye. I've uncovered cold hard facts that will lead me to one of the biggest salvage operations ever seen around these parts. It'll make your find look like something picked up by a weekend beach walker with a metal detector."

"That's great news. When you're filthy rich, us geezers won't hafta drive all the way to Jacksonville to pick you up."

"We weren't called geezers, you were. Don't include me," Nan scolded. "Jack, can I fix you something? I've stocked up on all of your favorites."

Despite the late hour, Nan looked like she was ready for a day out with friends. Her blonde hair, never out of place, helped give her the appearance of someone fifteen years younger. Pop joked that her youthfulness cost him three hundred bucks a month.

"Unless you have some of that datil pepper cornbread sitting around somewhere, I think I'm in good shape."

"Boy, you know Nan already has that cornbread baked and ready for you to inhale. I've been tryin' to get at it since it came outta the oven but had to wait 'til your sorry butt got here. You'd think you were the king of this castle 'stead of me."

Nan sighed patiently. "Don't pay him any mind. He's as spoiled as they come. I'll get you some Jack, and I guess I'll get some for the geezer here, along with his coffee." She kissed Pop lightly on the cheek. "How does that sound sweetheart?"

"Awwww I don't know. I can't afford to be puttin' on any weight. Don't forget, I'm about due for a peg leg any day now, 'least accordin' to old Calico Jack here."

Jack couldn't help but laugh at the banter. It was always the same and the winks and nods between his grandparents never stopped. They were like kids, totally devoted to one another. There was much to look forward to, old friends, the beach, the ancient city, and most of all, his very own boat, *Bad Latitude*.

True to form, Jack and Pop sat up for a few hours catching up on stories and discussing big plans for a couple of offshore fishing trips. The Kingfish were tearing it up just off the coast and the ten-day forecast was borderline fantastic. Pop thought it best to wait until midweek to *go after the big one*. He knew Jack would want to spend a couple of days looking up friends and spending time surfing off Crescent Beach. The fish would be ready for anything tossed their way. Jack trudged off to the boathouse just before daybreak to get some much-needed sleep. He smiled to himself, wondering if Pop would clean the Escalade before hitting the sack.

The home was situated on the Matanzas River, about a mile north of Crescent Beach. It was set back two hundred yards from the very scenic highway A1A, which separated the property from a thin strip of dunes running along the ocean. Pop had built the Spanish style house with an eye on entertaining and had included immense windows, high ceilings, and large spacious rooms with lots of ceiling fans. Nan had insisted on tile throughout with fancy moldings, window treatments, and finishes. The mix of glass, rattan, leather, and tropical themed paintings made each room unique and comfortably elegant. She was very fussy about her *tropicasual* look. The wrap around front porch with its thick columns created an inviting appearance. Behind the house was a huge screened porch where Pop's tiki bar was arranged to give guests a perfect view of sunsets beyond the waterway. A lanai covered the pool, which was surrounded by a series of waterfalls and lush tropical plants.

Pop had added a two-story boathouse and garage off the dock where the toys were kept. There were four hydraulic lifts under roof, used to keep the boats out of the water when not in use. In the outermost lift, Pop kept his thirty-eight foot Donzi that he had named *Laffin' Gaff*. Next to the Donzi was Nan's favorite, a blue and white custom-built Hurricane deck boat. The family used it to cruise the waterway, tow skiers, and anchor in small coves to swim and cook out on remote beaches. A pair of Jet Skis filled the space next to what Jack thought was the most spectacular boat on the water, *Bad Latitude*. It was his very own twenty-two foot Cobia center console, rigged with every possible option, including a high performance Yamaha 250 horsepower engine, bright blue T-Top with polished brass rocket launchers and a killer sound system. Pop had insisted that Jack take the Coast Guard boating classes the year before and surprised him with the boat on the very day he had passed the course. Jack's dad had not been amused by the extravagant gift but Nan had smoothed things over, as usual.

Covered inside the garage was Pop's pride and joy, a completely restored 1940 Chris-Craft wooden speedboat. Pop had named the boat *Deb's Temper* to placate Nan when it became clear that she wasn't very happy about the purchase. Through the garage, a set of stairs led to a spacious apartment above. Wood floors and rustic walls accented the space that was divided into a TV/game room, bedroom with bunk beds, and a small kitchen. On top of the boathouse, extending beyond the dock was a deck with picnic tables and lounge chairs made of teak wood. The deck was located out of direct view from the house, providing a hideout for Pop, where he would sneak off and puff his cigars, avoiding Nan's constant reminders of the health hazards of smoking.

It was the boathouse apartment where Jack stayed and hung out with friends. Nan and Pop had accessorized it with a huge flat screen TV, comfortable furnishings, XBox, PlayStation, and plenty of DVDs. Total responsible behavior was the non-negotiable rule for him and his friends to be allowed to use the rooms without strict supervision. This would be Jack's second summer living in the apartment as if it were his own and he would make sure that everyone behaved so that the privilege would not be lost.

2

Wave Riders

Jack left the house at eleven-fifteen following a huge breakfast and a *let's review the rules* chat with his grandparents. Wearing his favorite Billabong trunks, a sleeveless T-shirt and a pair of Reef flip-flops, he hustled out to the dock and hopped aboard a bright yellow Jet Ski. In a matter of minutes he was blasting south through the Matanzas Inlet into the ocean, and hooked a left turn north along the shoreline. At the midway point of his favorite surfing spot, he gently nudged the small watercraft into the shallows and secured it at the edge of the beach.

After vainly scouting the area for friends, Jack pushed the Jet Ski into the surf planning to run a few miles north toward the pier at St Augustine. As he climbed onto the watercraft, he was suddenly grabbed from below the surface, causing him to lose his balance and splash backwards under the waves. He was released just as his hands touched down on the sandy bottom and scrambled to his feet, coughing and sputtering on the salt water.

Jack was startled to find his best friend Kai, leaning casually against the Jet Ski with one arm draped across the seat. Kai carried a smug look as water cascaded down his face.

"You idiot," laughed Jack. "You almost gave me a heart attack."

"Yeah right, almost. Were you headin' somewhere lookin' for someone like me to pester?"

"I was hoping to avoid your ugly mug for the whole summer. How've you been Kai?"

Kai's parents, former professional surfers, had chosen the unique name leaving him the constant and annoying chore of explaining the pronunciation, which rhymed with sky.

"Things have been good Rackham. Can't complain any. Nan told me you were ridin' this way so I waited 'til you anchored up, so I could hide out and scare the crap outta you. I'm glad to see I haven't lost my touch, but you always were a wuss."

"Yeah right, so I'm a wuss. Where's everybody hanging out?"

"They're all up at Pelican Point, near my house. You wanna take a run up that way and get this party started?" Kai didn't wait for an answer and climbed onto the back of the Jet Ski.

"Sounds good to me."

They jetted through the surf until they reached the St. Augustine inlet, where Jack took a slight detour. Turning into the bay, they cruised alongside the ancient Spanish stronghold known as *Castillo de San Marcos*. The fortress was built in the

1600s by the Spanish to protect the city's citizens from attack during the days when Spain controlled Florida. Navigating through the maze of sailboats moored in the calm harbor, Jack noticed a girl with shiny blonde hair walking along the outer seawall of the fort, close to the water's edge. She was the prettiest girl he had ever laid eyes on and he couldn't help but gawk and smile. Her movements were graceful and carefree. She wore a strapless white outfit that showed off new tan lines, and, as the Jet Ski passed by, she offered a shy smile of her own and a tiny little wave, using only two fingers, acknowledging his attention.

"Look out you moron!" yelled Kai.

Jack faced forward just in time to see that they were on a collision course with a large wooden sailboat. A quick correction and too much throttle almost landed Kai in the bay.

"How 'bout I drive while *you* check out the scenery. I'd kinda like to live long enough to graduate. You can't drive with your head in your rear end."

"Did you see her?" stuttered Jack, oblivious to Kai's ranting. "Didja?"

"You mean the blonde walkin' along the wall? The one watchin' you makin' a total fool of yourself? Geez, I guess you're in love 'cause she smiled. How do you know she wasn't smilin' at me?"

"Why would she smile at a runt like you with those dreads and shabby shorts? You're even getting a blubber gut to go with that flabby looking chest."

There was nothing flabby about Kai, but Jack knew which buttons to push when he wanted to irritate. Kai was nearly a half-foot shorter but had a muscular build. Having lived on the island his entire life, his skin was deeply tanned and his dirty blonde, bleach streaked hair was curly enough to be mistaken for dreadlocks from a distance. His green eyes matched the color of the surf.

"I don't have an ounce of fat on me butthead. Let's go back and see who she was wavin' to."

"Nah, let's cruise to the point and see who's around. Like you said, let's get this party started."

Jack gunned the Jet Ski along and whizzed past the fort and the moored boats, cutting across the small bay. He was smiling, thinking about the girl walking on top of the wall. His first priority of the summer would be to find out all about her. If he had his way, it wasn't going to happen with Kai anywhere nearby. Hopefully she wasn't a tourist getting ready to return home.

Arriving at Vilano, the boys secured the watercraft on the bay side of Pelican Point and walked the short distance to the ocean. It didn't take long for Jack to be surrounded by a group of his old friends, all making suggestions about the best way to fill the rest of the day. Surfing topped the list and Kai jumped in a jeep with his buddy Caz to run back to the house to grab a couple of boards. Since Kai's parents owned the biggest surf shop on the island, he always had the latest and most high tech custom boards available. When he returned, Jack borrowed the Ocean Arrow and they kicked out to join the others. The waves were nothing special but the water was a warm eighty-four degrees and the sun was doing its best to burn through five layers of skin.

For three hours, it was like old times. The surf was crowded and there were plenty of decent rides. Between sets, they hung out on the boards, making jokes and busting on one another with good-natured insults.

Grant, a gangly sixteen-year-old, paddled over to the group. Jack was busy describing the girl at the Castillo to his longtime friends, Valerie and Nina. "We're gonna roll down to

Crescent Beach later. You guys are gonna to be there, right?" interrupted a hopeful Grant as he eyed the girls.

Kai spoke up for everyone. "Yeah, 'round seven o'clock, we'll be there."

"I can't make it until later. I'm going to see if a friend of mine can come," answered Val.

Nina looked puzzled. "What friend are you talking about?"

"I think Talia might want to party with us, but she already told me she was going to be busy until about nine."

Jack was curious. "Who's Talia?"

"Nina, we have to get going or we're gonna miss our ride," giggled Val. She paddled away, totally ignoring his question.

Jack shrugged it off. "Kai, these waves are starting to suck. I need to get going anyway so I can get the Jet Ski back. You stopping by the house or are we meeting at the beach?"

"I'll meet you at the beach. I'm gonna hang for a little longer. Throw the board in Caz' jeep for me." Kai was staring in Val's direction as she stroked her way toward shore.

Jack carried the board to the Jeep and carefully leaned it against the padded roll bar in the back. He walked around to the point, hopped on the Jet Ski, and was on his way down the coast. Thirty minutes later, he docked on the floating platform below the boathouse and climbed the ladder.

After a quick shower, a change of clothes, and a couple of sandwiches, Jack walked down the brick pathway toward the garage. Sago palms, banana trees, and tropical plants of all shapes and colors lined the walk and patio. Nan took great pride in her gardens. They provided plenty of backdrops for her photography hobby. Several of her photos had been published in local and national magazines. Jack recalled a time when she captured a pygmy rattler in a juice container, to get close up shots of its markings and colors. She sent the pictures to one of Jack's cranky aunts when the aunt was trying to mooch an invitation for a visit. The talk of a visit ended abruptly, much to Nan's relief.

Pop was in the garage tinkering with his fishing tackle while secretly puffing away on what he would call a collector's item cigar. Jack didn't know much about cigars, only that they smelled lousy and Nan complained whenever Pop lit one up.

"What's up Pop?"

"Just tryin' to make sure that everything's ship shape so we're not out on the water pokin' 'round searchin' for the one rig that might snag this year's big one pal."

Jack chuckled. He knew Pop was all talk about the *big one*. The truth was, Pop wasn't much of a fisherman, despite the fancy equipment and rigging. His grandfather always enjoyed taking friends and family out, but spent most of his time aboard playing captain and first mate so everyone else would have fun. When teased about his normally bad fishing luck, he would offer a myriad of excuses before grudgingly admitting that it was Nan who had the real knack for the sport.

"Pop, I was studying some stuff about the massacre at the Matanzas Inlet back in1565 and I think there's a good chance there may be some shipwrecks nearby. The French were trying to get control of St. Augustine and this guy Jean something…"

"Ribault" interrupted Pop. "His name was Jean Ribault and he led six hundred men from France to what was then known as La Florida to reinforce Fort Caroline, up there in Jacksonville, so the Frenchys could take over entire the territory from Spain. He was on a mission to attack St. Augustine when a hurricane wiped out his fleet of ships."

"Right, and while the French were trying to attack St. Augustine, the Spanish took over Fort Caroline." Jack was getting warmed up now.

"I don't want to bust your bubble kid, but those ships were blown way off course and wrecked near Daytona and Cape Canaveral. Besides, I doubt they would have carried anything of value on an attack mission. The inlet only became famous because of the slaughter. The French soldiers that survived the shipwreck, were on foot tryin' to get back to Ft. Caroline when the Spaniards intercepted them and massacred them there at the inlet. The word Matanzas actually means place of slaughters. Admiral Pedro Menendez de Aviles led the attack. I'm sure you've heard that name before."

"That's the name of Kai's high school, *Pedro Menendez*. Why would they name a school after someone that slaughtered a bunch of people?"

"First of all," explained Pop patiently, "Menendez was only defending the territory. He was the founder of St. Augustine. The school is named after the founder, not for what happened at the inlet."

Jack was disappointed. He thought he had picked up a lead on buried treasure and Pop had shot down his theory with some basic history within minutes.

"Jack, it's like I told you, when treasure hunting, historical clues are studied as part of an entire puzzle. All of the pieces have to fit. Any inaccuracy, even a minor detail, can throw you way off course. You're not far off the mark though when you suspect that particular area for a stash of loot. Once you had settled in I'd planned on runnin' an idea past you, to see if you'd be interested in tryin' your hand at a real search."

"You kidding me Pop? That's my all time dream."

"Well, we'll have to map it all out and you look like you've got somethin' already planned. Let's get together in a few days when the dust settles. Now, just so you know, my part in this little escapade is to advise only. You're gonna to have to track the clues and do the work. I'm also assumin' you're gonna need some help, so your friend Kai is probably gonna need to be part of this."

"As long as that's okay with you, sure," answered Jack.

"It's okay with me or I wouldn't have suggested it. He's a good kid, even if he does have weird hair. The most important thing to remember is you gotta keep your mouths shut. Don't be blabbin' it all over town or every nerd with a metal detector will be crawlin' all over the place."

"This is totally awesome Pop. How long have you been sitting on this?"

"Oh, 'bout 10 years."

"Why didn't you go after it yourself and why didn't you tell me about this before?"

"I've already had my fair share of adventure and made plenty of money while I was at it. I was savin' this 'til I thought you could handle it. I think you're ready now. It's time for you to get into the Rackham treasure huntin' game. Anyway, you'd better get your butt in gear and get goin'. We'll talk later, when I'm not so busy putterin' around." Pop looked at Jack with a mischievous smile. "Now you know why we live here. I had to keep an eye on your gold."

"Why can't we do it now?"

"You've got somewhere to go and there's a lot of stuff that I'll need to explain."

"I don't have to go. It's just a party on the beach. We do that all summer."

"Okay, then let's just say I want the suspense to build." Pop waved him away and turned back toward the tackle scattered on the bench top, signaling Jack that the conversation was over.

Jack knew better than to pry anymore and left the garage to begin his short walk to the beach. Smiling at the thought of his own chance at a real search for gold, he wondered just how long Pop would make him wait before sharing the clues and details.

He reached the access ramp to the beach and walked south past the condos toward an already blazing fire. There were several Jeeps and jacked up four by four trucks parked along the bottom of the dunes. Jack always joked that his friends' rides were *red necked up* because of the oversized tires and loud exhaust systems. As he approached the group, he wondered how long it would take the St John's County Sheriff's Department to pay them all a visit. The sheriffs were usually cool, and, with the exception of a few exercise freaks, the kids would have the beach all to themselves.

Jack & Talia

3

Beach Party

"Hey Rackham! What's up?"

It was Jack's friend Eric stepping from behind a silver Ford F-150. He was a year older and, though they were about the same height, he outweighed Jack by nearly sixty pounds. For the past two summers, Eric had worked for his uncle, installing cabinets and trim work in new houses, putting in as many hours as possible earning money for college. Getting a football scholarship to play for the Florida Gators was Eric's dream, but he knew it wasn't a sure bet. Stockpiling funds now would be a huge help for his parents, as the cost for tuition, books, and living expense was not easily affordable for a family with seven kids.

"Looks like you've been hitting the gym more than usual," Jack replied as the two friends smiled and bumped knuckles in greeting.

"Yeah, I work upper body one night, legs the next. I'm trying to get my body fat below six per cent to make sure I'm in shape for the start of football camp."

"Well, no offense, but you need to add getting a tan to your list of things to do. You're looking like a tourist," laughed Jack.

"You've got that right, but I've been jammed. This is my first time on the beach since March."

"Being here at night isn't gonna get you any tanner," Jack teased.

"No, guess not, but hey, really, it's great to see you. Hopefully, I can get some time off so we can hang out. I brought five buckets of shrimp and my dad's steamer pots. Trace's Mom is sending over a bunch of burgers and hot dogs. How about giving me a hand getting this stuff spread out." Eric turned and began unloading the truck.

The shrimp were huge, caught that very morning, and had been kept on ice all day for the party. As the water came to a boil, Jack snapped the heads off and tossed the shrimp into the large steamers. Caz and Kai arrived, late as usual, with four charcoal grills strapped to Caz' jeep. There was no small talk as they went to work setting them up.

While the shrimp steamed away, Kai played master chef, keeping track of the burgers and hot dogs, and Jack and the others pitched in with other chores. It was a bit past nine when they were visited by one of the deputies. They nicknamed him Deputy Dan and invited him to stop by later to grab some grub before his shift ended. The deputy warned everyone to keep the noise down so as not to annoy the people living along that stretch of beach. If the homeowners complained, he would have no choice but to shut the party down and chase them all for the night. No one wanted to risk being bounced.

Several Jeeps were parked facing a volleyball net. All of them were rigged with racks of KC lights mounted above the windshields and would be used to light up the playing area.

The food was awesome, and the jokes and insults were flying back and forth, nonstop. Grant was the best storyteller of the bunch and everyone knew that everything out of his mouth was probably true. His crazy family was always his favorite topic. When he imitated his chubby redneck uncle Ferdie, everyone howled until they cried. As Grant explained, Ferdie was supposed to be a Freddie, but Grandma wasn't much of a speller. After the rough start, it was only downhill from there for his poor old uncle and the rest of the clan.

While laughing along with friends, Jack spied a trio of girls sauntering their way toward the group. It was impossible to make out who they were, since he was staring from the area lit up by the Jeeps and into the darkness. He might not have noticed at all had the moon not been so bright. As the girls stepped into the lighted area, Jack realized it was Val, Nina and the girl from the Castillo. *It has to be that friend that Val was hinting about. She must have figured out who I was describing when we were waiting to catch waves.* His face turned crimson at the thought, remembering how he had gushed to Val about the girl on the seawall. With his imagination running wild, trying to remember exactly what was said, he found himself wishing for a place to hide. Valerie would enjoy seeing him squirm while she introduced her friend.

Jack's panic was interrupted by a movement to his left. He turned to see Kai pointing and gesturing like a fifth grader. This was awful, and meeting someone with Kai being in the same zip code was even worse. There was nothing that satisfied

Kai more than embarrassing him when they were around girls. For some reason, Kai never worried about looking stupid or immature. Girls liked him anyway, always telling him he was *so cute*. Jack wished he'd brought the Jet Ski for a quick getaway.

Val pranced and wiggled to within inches of where he was sitting. "Hi Jack, I thought you might like to meet a very good friend of mine." She had a devilish gleam in her eye that confirmed the worst of his fears. He knew, without any doubt, that she had already described how he had enthusiastically gushed about the gorgeous looking blonde girl from *The Castillo*. There were no rocks to hide under and no help in site. He would have to suck it up and play along.

Jack took on the casual, confident approach as he smiled. "Hi Val, it's nice of you to rush past everyone else just to see me. I assume this is your friend that was busy 'til after nine." He was thankful to be sitting. His legs felt like linguini.

Val charged ahead, ignoring the sarcasm; "This is Talia. You were telling me *all* about her when we were surfing today. I told her how desperate you were to meet her and how you thought she was absolutely beautiful."

Jack groaned inside. Val was enjoying this for all it was worth and he wasn't getting off the hook. He had to dig deep to appear sure of himself.

Turning toward Talia, making his best attempt at a smile, his mock confidence melted. The lights from the jeeps made it look as though she was standing in brilliant sunlight. *Deep Blue Eyes.* They were as blue as any pool he had ever seen. He was completely locked onto those incredible eyes, and now his mouth was moving wordlessly trying to introduce himself. This was heading down the tubes in a hurry and Kai was walking toward them, which would only make things worse. He had to get it together fast.

"Hi Talia. I'm Jack, as I'm sure Val managed to mention, while exaggerating absolutely everything I may have said earlier. For what it's worth, don't believe any of it."

Whew, that was tough, and just in time. Hope she didn't pick up on that little tap dance. At least I didn't stutter or get my own name wrong.

Talia smiled. "I remember waving to you from the wall at the old fort this morning when you were riding the Jet Ski."

Jack felt his face redden again as Kai stepped in "Yeah an' he almost got us killed 'cause he was busy starin' at you."

Geez. This is out of control.

"Well, it's nice to meet you. Just ignore him. He was just released from the psyche ward, and they forgot to give him his meds," interrupted Jack, now clearly annoyed.

"Don't let these guys get to you. I'm sorry you didn't stop," answered Talia.

Jack stood to his full height next to the much shorter Kai. "I might have if I didn't have this pint sized Bob Marley with me."

"You're a riot, jerk weed," Kai snapped. Jack couldn't be sure if he had taken exception to being called pint sized or Bob Marley. Kai stomped off before he could find out, but knew he would hear about it later.

Things were loosening up and Jack's confidence was returning. Talia knew this was Val's set up but was determined to make things as relaxed as possible. This guy Jack was even cuter up close, with a kind, intelligent face and a nice smile. She loved the way he had focused on her eyes. Now if they could get away from the nosy crowd for a little while, maybe they could get to know one another.

Val jumped in breaking off the stare. "Talia's here visiting her aunt for the whole summer. She's from Los Angeles and has a brother and sister. Her Dad builds big buildings and she's seen all kinds of famous actors and goes to…"

Talia laughed nervously as she cut her off. "Okay Val, he doesn't need my family history." She turned again toward Jack. He was nearly a foot taller and an amused expression was plastered across his face. "You don't feel like hearing all of this, right?"

"Well, yeah, I'd kinda like to hear it, but maybe we can wait 'til we don't have an audience," said Jack as he motioned toward Val with a *get lost* nod.

Talia laughed again, she was going to like this guy. She felt completely at ease.

Val announced with a huff that she was going to visit her other friends and moved off to where Kai and Nina were hanging out.

"So, what do you feel like doing? The food's good, I can take you around so you can meet my friends, whatever you want," he suggested.

"I think we should take a walk, if you don't mind. It's not like I know anyone here and it would give us a chance to start over without everybody hanging out to listen. Is that okay with you?"

Jack laughed. "Sure. Besides, I could use a break from you know who."

Talia smiled again. Out of the corner of her eye, she spotted Val and Nina giggling and blowing kisses in her direction from several yards away. "Let's go for that walk. I feel like I'm part of a freak show."

They walked toward the inlet, spending the time making small talk about summer plans, surfing, their likes, and dislikes. The sea was calm and as the moon reflected off the surface, it seemed to follow them all along the water's edge.

Amazingly, they discovered they had a number of things in common, the oddest being the same birth date, with Jack being four hours younger. He explained that it could present a problem, as his mom would never approve of him being involved with an *older* woman. That bit of wit earned him a playful elbow to the ribs, a reach for the much shorter Talia.

An hour later, they returned to the now curious group and Jack introduced Talia to everyone, including a still sulking Kai. After eating their fill of shrimp and mixing with new and old friends, it was time to call it a night. Before parting company, they punched each other's cell number into their phones, promising to get together again within a few days. Jack wondered who would call first, deep down knowing he would be the first to cave in.

4

The Diary of Solomon Cresson

"Rise n' shine, it's you, me, *Laffin' Gaff* and the deep blue sea," hollered Pop as he banged on Jack's door. It was a startling way to wake up.

Jack mumbled something, letting his grandfather know he would be out in a minute. He dressed in dark blue Columbia shorts and a pale yellow shirt. After stepping into a pair of well-worn deck shoes, he grabbed his Freestyle dive watch and shuffled through the door toward the back of the main house. Nan was waiting with two small coolers and a thermos filled with hot coffee.

"Hustle up kid, can't keep the old boy waiting." She reached to hand Jack the coolers. "The light blue one has breakfast sandwiches that are nice and hot so don't wait too long to eat them."

Smiling through a yawn, he gave Nan a one armed hug and a peck on the cheek. "Thanks, Nan, we'll eat them on the way down river. I'm starved."

Jack scurried down the dock and noticed that *Laffin' Gaff* had been lowered into the water and the three high-powered engines were already running. Handing the coolers and thermos over the side
to Pop, he jumped aboard, moving forward to remove the tether from the bow cleat. Before letting the spring line loose, he and Pop went through a final checklist, making sure nothing was forgotten. At five-thirty, they were underway.

"So Pop, are you going to tell me today where that treasure is?"

"Yeah, maybe later. There's some stuff I gotta show you when we get around to that. Let's enjoy some fishin' first."

There was a slight mist and the morning air felt damp. Pop, being as picky as he was, had wiped the boat down so that everything gleamed. Jack wondered if the man ever slept. After pouring the coffee and grabbing the sandwiches, he joined Pop at the helm. He always enjoyed these trips and was anxious to get *Laffin' Gaff* cranked up. Neither had much to say while they ate their breakfast and motored toward the ocean. The mist would burn off as the sun continued to rise.

Once Pop navigated the treacherous sandbar stretching across the Matanzas Inlet, he threw the throttles forward and the boat planed out quickly to speed across the calm blue water. They were running at forty-five knots north by northeast in search of the shrimping fleet. It took less than twenty minutes for the giant wing-like outriggers to come into view.

On their approach to the shrimp boats, Pop cut the engines back to idle and yelled, "Awright, weight 'em n' bait 'em", and they began the chore of attaching two-ounce weights and large mullet to their rigs. Taking care to avoid the nets, Pop eased the powerful Donzi behind the cluster of boats and they cast the baited lines into the sea several yards behind the last in line. For the next couple of hours they were caught up in the non-stop action, catching and releasing a mix of Kingfish, Wahoo, and Cobia.

At the first sign of a slow down, they abandoned the fleet, moving west to try their luck over top of some wrecks, trying to pull a couple of Grouper to take home. Nan loved blackened Grouper and reminded Pop that her iron skillet would be waiting when they returned. As noon approached, the light breeze disappeared and the heat became intense. That was enough for Pop to call it a day and head back to port with a single large keeper fish in the box. On the ride in, Jack decided the timing was perfect to pick Pop's brain about the ten-year-old secret.

"So Pop, can you maybe start telling me about where you think the gold is hidden?"

"Guess you're gettin' anxious now huh. How 'bout I go through all of that as soon as we get home n' cleaned up. There's some stuff I gotta show you."

Jack could hardly contain his excitement. They would be dockside within the hour and he would finally have what he needed to start his own treasure hunt. As they made the turn up river toward the boathouse, he gathered the gear and prepared the temporary tie lines. Within minutes, Pop was reversing the engines to align the Donzi with the boatlift. The engines were shut down and tilted forward and *Laffin' Gaff* was lifted gently from the water. They went about the business of getting everything scrubbed down and put away in record time and Pop cleaned the Grouper as Jack stowed the tackle and fishing poles.

"Why don't you go ahead and get showered up. I'll meet you in my study in thirty minutes."

"I can be ready in ten."

"Well, I'll need a bit longer than that Sonny, so hold your horses and plan on bein' in my study around two."

"Alright. Do you need help with anything else?"

"Nah, go ahead. We're shipshape here. I'm gonna get this fish in the house so Nan can do her thing and I'll catch up with you shortly."

Jack hurried through his shower and rushed into the house to Pop's study, parking himself in one of the large leather chairs in front of a huge desk. Pop had crafted the desk himself, using the parts of a salvaged helm from a steamer ship that had sunk more than one hundred years earlier. The study was lined with shelves stocked with hundreds of books and Jack was sure that Pop had read all of them at least twice. In the corner stood a huge drawing table covered with charts and maps. At the window, overlooking the Matanzas River, was a highly polished mahogany and brass trimmed binnacle from a nineteenth century sailing sloop, protecting an equally impressive lighted compass.

Pop entered the room ten minutes later and, ignoring Jack momentarily, marched directly toward a built in cabinet at the center of the wall. Unlocking the cabinet, he carefully removed a worn looking leather book and ambled over to his desk. Once comfortably adjusted in his seat, he opened the book and removed a fragile yellowed parchment that had been folded many times. He spread it out on the glass covered wood surface of the massive desk.

"Do you remember a few years ago when we camped at Jonathan Dickinson State Park?" Pop began very deliberately.

"Yeah, sure. It was an awesome trip. I was eleven or twelve."

"Well, before I tell you where you should search, it's important for you to hear a bit of the history. I want you to have an appreciation for what happened back in the day when this treasure was hidden. The whole story is right here," Pop explained as he patted the leather of the old diary. He shared the ancient tale from memory while Jack listened intently.

"In 1696, sailing from Jamaica to Philadelphia, a Quaker named Jonathan Dickinson was traveling on a ship named *The Reformation*. During a vicious hurricane on the twenty fourth of September, the vessel was wrecked off the coast, near what is now known as Jupiter Inlet. The survivors abandoned the derelict ship and made camp along the beach where the park now sits. Soon after making landfall, they were ambushed by local natives who threatened their lives, stole their few remaining provisions, and abused them severely. What people today would call Indian Chiefs were actually Kings, known then as the *Cacique*. Several weeks following their capture, they were released and instructed to travel north. The weary, starving group traveled for nearly two months toward St. Augustine, without sufficient food, water, or shelter."

"Prior to the initial encounter with the locals, now documented to be the Jobe tribe, one of the crew, Solomon Cresson, secretly stashed a box of gold coins and gemstones, behind some dunes. Fortunately, for Mr. Cresson, the tribesman thought he was a troublemaker so he was ordered to proceed alone. This gave Cresson the chance to collect his hidden prize, undetected by the others, and smuggle the booty north past the Matanzas Inlet. Once there, he buried the treasure in a freshly dug Indian grave, because he was afraid it would be confiscated by the Spaniards when he reached *Castillo de San Marcos*. The surviving passengers finally joined him in St. Augustine a few of weeks later but he kept the secret, planning to return one day to collect his gold."

"The Spanish nursed the travelers back to health and gave them provisions for the long trek to Charles Town. There, they boarded a ship bound for Philadelphia, ending an ordeal that had lasted nearly five months. Five members of the party had died along the way from starvation or exposure."

"Solomon Cresson never returned to claim his treasure. Failing health caused him to give up his profession as a mariner and he settled in a small town outside of Philadelphia, working as a printer. This old leather bound book is his personal diary describing the events of those difficult months, along with this crude map and description of the area where the loot is hidden."

"So how did you get the diary?" asked Jack.

"Well, I grew up near the town where Mr. Cresson lived out his final days. When I was young, my grandfather enjoyed goin' to weekend auctions and he always took me along." Pop laughed. "I got my first dog, by mistake I might add, at one of those auctions. I didn't know that raising your hand meant you were bidding. Anyway, I was about six years old and they were auctioning off these old books, a whole box of 'em. My grandfather was the tenth child in a household of fifteen kids. Education wasn't thought to be so important in those days and his parents made him quit school to get a job and help support the family. He never even finished fourth grade. Anyway, he felt bad about his lack of education so he was always interested in how I was doin' in school. He bought the books for a dollar and gave 'em to me so I would, as he said, *learn readin' real good.* I still have some of those old books, but this one's special. The last entry is from 1733. Some of it's difficult to understand because of the old fashioned use of the English language." Pop carefully turned the pages and stared at the book, while memories of his own grandfather flooded his thoughts. Jack thought he noticed Pop's eyes tearing up.

After a full minute, Pop cleared his throat. "I remembered the story in this book after we moved here and finally put two n' two together. The leather was torn a little on the bottom edge and the corner of this paper was peekin' out. I opened the frayed area as carefully as I dared and pulled out this map. It shows a mark where three rivers join together northwest of the inlet. In his notes, Cresson mentioned the sitting guards. That was another clue. Around the time of the shipwreck, the native inhabitants buried their dead in sitting positions. I figured out where it was and walked the area ten years ago, pokin' around for a couple of weeks. The remnants of an Indian grave were pretty much where the map showed it. I decided then and there to wait until you were older to share this with you." Pop leaned back in the chair silently studying his grandson's awestruck expression.

Jack's mind was racing, picturing himself finding and uncovering the treasure buried at the three rivers. He knew it was behind old Fort Matanzas, near one of his favorite fishing spots.

"Do you really think I can do it?"

"Yeah, I do, but it won't be easy. The first thing you have to understand is that your work has to be carefully disguised, so boaters and fishermen don't get suspicious and the secret gets blown outta

the water. Don't invite problems. Oh, and keep this in mind, it's in an ancient burial ground and I've heard stories about strange stuff going on whenever the earth is disturbed in those places."

"Well, maybe we could make up a game plan Pop."

"What I want you to do is make up your own plan. I'll eyeball it and try to shoot holes in it. This has to be your adventure with me actin' as the advisor and stayin' in the background."

"Okay, that sounds fair. Can I borrow the book and map and get started right away?"

"Jackson, this belongs to you now. As far as I'm concerned, this is part of the treasure and I want you to have it. You can pass it down to your own grandson someday."

Jack felt a lump in his throat. He couldn't reply, barely managing to nod his head up and down, as he understood the enormity of the gift he had been given. Pop stood, patted Jack firmly on the shoulder, and left the study without another word.

Alone and settled, Jack began hatching his strategy. The most serious obstacle was how to excavate while disguising the work. He decided there was no choice but to search during daylight and document the search grid using a handheld GPS. The work could be concealed by saving the marsh grasses to patch over the spots where they probed, but the actual dig, to claim the Cresson treasure, would have to be done in the dark of night.

Jack returned to the boathouse apartment, spending the remainder of the afternoon alone, struggling to interpret the diary and map while comparing the ancient information with current charts of the waterway and the island.

It was getting late when he finally took a break from his planning. It was as good a time as any to give Talia a call. He would ask if she and Val would like to take a boat ride tomorrow. Kai had been bugging him to take *Bad Latitude* for a spin since his arrival. He smiled, thinking about how impressed Talia would be once she realized that the boat belonged to him. Grabbing the cell phone from the pocket of his cargo shorts, he leaned back in the recliner and dialed her number.

5

Bad Latitude

Jack and Kai were dockside when Val and Talia arrived. Nan greeted them warmly and showed them through from the entry foyer. Val had known Nan and Pop for about five years and had been to the house several times before, so she felt right at home. Talia was blown away by the house and the property, but was even more impressed with how welcome Nan had made her feel. Val had given her a brief heads up about the estate-like property but the description didn't prepare her for what she was seeing. Jack never mentioned anything about the place. He had called the night before asking if she and Val would like to take a boat ride and now she found herself walking toward the dock, past all kinds of exotic plants and shrubs. It reminded her, in a way, of the gardens at *The Jax Zoo*, but on a smaller scale. The boathouse was another shock. It looked like someone could live there. She could see Kai yapping away animatedly and Jack, standing in the boat, laughing and shaking his head.

Talia could hear Jack as she approached. "Is there anything you don't complain about?"

"All I'm sayin' is we should take some poles and some tackle and try our luck for a little while. Why waste a trip jus' ridin' around?" whined Kai.

"I didn't ask them if they wanted to go fishing. All I said was let's go for a ride. I don't think.... Hi Talia. Val. Guess we're ready to go whenever you guys give us the word."

Talia stared down at the boat. The name *Bad Latitude,* in multi colored decals, was displayed prominently in detailed script along the side of the spotless white hull. A cooler and a large bag filled with towels were stored on the deck at the bow and music blared from speakers hidden somewhere below the T-top. She thought Jack looked hot, especially with his shirt off and caught herself staring at his muscular chest and arms. A pair of jet black Oakleys hid his bright blue eyes and she blushed, worried that he may have noticed her stare.

"Well, whaddya gonna do, waste the day gawkin' or you gonna climb aboard?" grumped Kai. Suddenly his face brightened. "Hey, do you guys want to do some fishin'?"

"Fishin'? I don't want to get all smelly. Jack asked if we wanted to go for a ride," protested Val firmly.

"No fishing today. I thought it might be cool to take a run to Jacksonville and maybe swing by St. Augustine on the way back. Let's just cruise around today. We can stop at a cove somewhere for lunch or maybe dock up at a place called The Landing in downtown Jax," answered Jack good-naturedly. He could see Talia's relieved expression and removed the shades in time to wink as he smiled.

Kai resumed his pouting as his final hope for a fishing trip evaporated.

"Are you allowed to use *this* boat?" asked Talia.

A still cranky Kai answered in his snottiest tone before Jack could reply. "Of course we can use *this* boat. This is *his* boat; the other ones belong to his Pop."

Talia was annoyed and looked toward Jack accusingly. "Wait a minute. You're telling me that *you own* this boat?"

"No. I'm not telling you I own this boat. Kai told you I owned this boat." Jacks' face was flushed with a mix embarrassment and annoyance.

"So do you?"

"Do I what?"

"Do you own this boat?"

"Yeah, I own this boat. Is there some problem with that?"

As usual, Kai broke in sarcastically, still peeved at not getting his way. "Would you two just get in the boat so we can shove off? He owns the boat. He knows how to run the boat. There's gas in the boat, food in the boat, life jackets in the boat and the two of us in the boat. If you guys would get in the boat, then everything and everybody would be in the boat. We could leave, and then all of us can *talk* about the boat, if that's what y'all wanna do. The day will be shot while we all stand around here blabbin'. C'mon, can we just go now?"

The girls tiptoed their way onboard and shuffled forward to the bow. Val, knowing Kai so well, thought the exchange was funny, vintage Kai, but Talia was embarrassed and felt out of place. She now privately wished that she had turned the invitation down. Jack, sensing her discomfort, suggested she ride at the helm with him. He hoped to explain that Kai was just being Kai and meant no harm. With a very terse nod, *no* she joined Val on the seat at the bow while Jack fired up the engine.

Jack reversed *Bad Latitude* from the slip and within minutes, they were running at full throttle through the Matanzas. The water and weather conditions were perfect and

Jack's pride and joy was running better than ever. During the early part of the ride, he tried several times to make eye contact with Talia but she went out of her way to ignore him and he finally gave up. They cruised past St. Augustine into the Tolomato River, beyond the Guana River State Park, and behind Jacksonville Beach.

Reaching a small bay, Jack abruptly slowed to trolling speed. Talia noticed that he spent much of the time checking a little screen mounted above the wheel at the helm. Worried that disaster might be in the works; she put her damaged pride aside and moved next to him to see for herself. "Is something wrong? You've slowed way down and keep looking at that thingy on the dashboard."

"Everything's almost fine. I'm watching the depth that's all. This is Chicopit Bay and it's very shallow. I have to make sure we stay in the channel and keep plenty of water under us so we don't run aground." There was no edge to his voice or any trace of concern. "The *thingy* that I'm looking at is a combination depth finder, which uses sonar to track the depth of the water, and a GPS, which stands for Global Positioning System. The GPS uses satellites to track where we are. Setting different points in the system and then monitoring the screen will show me how to get where I want to go or how to get back to where I started," he explained patiently.

"Wow. High tech. I guess I have a lot to learn about boats. Why did you say almost fine? Is there some other problem?"

"I'm just trying to figure out how to get Kai to keep his yap shut and how to keep you from paying attention to him when he runs his mouth. He gets carried away sometimes but don't forget, he's used to just the two of us running around talking trash to each other. Mr. Sensitive he's not. If you're too thin-skinned, he'll get on your nerves in a hurry."

"I guess I thought you guys were trying to make fun of me while you tried to convince me that you really owned this incredible boat."

"If I told you I didn't own the boat would that make you feel any better?"

"No, Val already told me it was yours, and that your grandfather bought it for you. She also said I have to chill when it comes to Kai; sometimes he gets kind of obnoxious. By the way, I think she really likes him."

"Well, between you and me, Kai's had a thing for her for a couple years. He tries to act like a tough guy, but he's really crazy about her. It's funny the way he always makes sure she's watching any time he gets on top of a nice wave or gets big air on a kite board. I'm not kidding. You watch next time we hit the beach."

"Yeah, look at them. She's chattering away, blinking those big lashes at him and he's staring back at her while he cracks his knuckles over and over. He's a love struck nervous wreck."

Talia settled into the swivel seat next to where Jack was standing. *This is good. He really is a nice guy, not a show off.*

Soon they were moving south into the St. Johns River past the port and massive cargo ships, and entered the city of Jacksonville a little before noon. Talia noticed that Jack took great care to keep track of the boat traffic around them while observing the markers and postings along the channel. Crossing under the bridges into downtown, past the tall condos and high-rise buildings was exciting. Even Kai seemed psyched, especially when Jack pointed the boat toward a large building with a bright orange roof and a sign reading *The Landing*. Approaching a concrete bulkhead, Jack throttled *Bad Latitude's* engine back and spun the nose of the boat in the opposite direction.

"Kai, tie a couple of those fenders on the starboard side, we're gonna dock up here for a while," ordered Jack as he positioned the vessel for docking.

"There you go again with your sea captain talk. Now what does starboard mean?"

"Starboard means, as we face forward from inside the boat, like this, the right side. When I say port, it means left. The bow is the front of the boat and the stern is the back. I just told Kai to hang the fenders, which are heavy plastic inflated tubes, from the starboard side because that's the side of the boat that will be up against the bulkhead when dock. The fenders work like rubber bumpers to keep the hull and rails from getting scraped while we're tied up." He seemed to enjoy explaining how things worked.

"How do you know all this stuff?" questioned a newly impressed Talia.

"Well, I've spent a lot of time on boats with my Pop, since I was just a little guy. He even made me take the Coast Guard course. In a couple years I'm gonna take the Captain's test, and then you'll have to call me 'Cap'n Jack' and salute me."

"That's soooo cool. Maybe you can dress up like a pirate and walk around with a bird on your shoulder," giggled Talia.

"Now you're talking. Believe it or not, I'm a descendant of a nasty old pirate. Jack Rackham was a buccaneer back in the early 1700s. He married Anne Bonny, one of only a few female pirates in those days. History says she was more ruthless than most of the men, and a much better fighter. So that's where all of us Rackhams come from. If you like pirates, we'll take the trip to Fernandina one day. You'll see some real pirate history up there."

"Is that where your family, uh, got all their money?" Talia was immediately embarrassed as the question escaped her lips. It seemed Jack had gone out of his way to downplay his family's awesome wealth and now she felt like she was being rude.

Jack laughed. "You're funny when you get flustered. No, we didn't inherit anything if that's what you mean. Pop researched the family tree and discovered our roots years ago. Studying the history of pirates became one of his many interests and that led to his treasure hunting, where he made lots of money. Jack Rackham actually died penniless. He was captured by the English and taken to Gallows Point in Jamaica in 1720 where he was executed. Anne Bonny was captured at the same time but, because she was going to have a baby, was released. She returned to her father's plantation in North Carolina where she gave birth to her only son, Jacob. Since the day old Calico Jack was strung up, the family has been a hard working, law abiding bunch of crazies, as far as I know anyway."

"Is that why your grandfather flies that pirate flag on the boathouse?"

"Yep. That's the Rackham flag, a skull with crossed swords, also called cutlasses. All of the pirates had their own flags, kind of like personal logos. Pop has it painted on the tailgate of his truck too. Nan says it looks ridiculous but he likes to aggravate her. He's always telling her that he's got to fly the family colors."

"You're really telling the truth?"

"Absolutely. Just ask Nan."

Talia let the subject drop as Jack glided alongside the seawall. Kai yelled out that the fenders were set and jumped up behind the bow rail to secure the boat to a docking cleat.

Within minutes, they were tied off at the bulkhead in front of an open square. The plaza was lined with restaurants, stores, and quaint little shops. Music pulsed through the shopping area from a bandstand strategically placed in the center of the square. On the river-walk, they visited stores, checked out other boats, and watched as the city's water taxi made several trips from west side to east and back again. Kai had plenty of witty, but mostly unkind insults about the landlubber tourists getting on and off.

Jack pulled on a black tee shirt. "Shrimp sounds good to me. How about you guys?"

"We goin' to Harry's Place?" asked Kai.

"Unless someone has a better suggestion, I'm in the mood for some southern fried shrimp with hush puppies and sweet tea."

Talia couldn't resist, "Okay Cap'n, so continue my education. What's a hush puppy?"

Kai jumped in to explain that it was a deep fried ball of corn dough with a salty sweet taste. He was doing his best to be extra nice and polite.

Val and Talia looked at each other and smiled. They had no idea that lunch at a waterside table would be part of their ride. Talia noticed Kai whispering something to Jack who was smiling, and nodding his head, trying to be low key. She wondered what it was that they had up their sleeves.

Lunch turned out to be a seafood feast. Everyone ordered something different and then shared, dividing fried, steamed, and blackened shrimp, broiled crab cakes, grilled Mahi, and a triple order of hush puppies. The check came and the guys split the tab. Talia thought it was cute when Kai eyed Val as he put his cash in with Jack's and decided that that had been what Kai had been whispering about earlier.

"Do you think the boat will hold us all now after all of that food?" asked Val as they headed down the walkway. They all complained good-naturedly about how they felt ready to bust.

"There's a restroom over there on the left. Now would be a good time to visit before we shove off," suggested Kai.

Talia was grateful for the suggestion. It wasn't like they were only a few minutes from home. Val giggled and patted Kai on the cheek for being so smart and thoughtful. Jack rolled his eyes and shrugged toward Talia as the girls trotted off toward the ladies room.

Jack looked toward Kai. "Maybe we should hit the head ourselves. It's a long ride." He turned to walk toward the men's room. "By the way, when did you become such a gentleman?"

"Whaddya mean? I can't be nice once in a while?"

"You weren't such a nice guy before we left."

"Yeah, I know. Sorry 'bout that. I was kinda nervous and thought this was really gonna suck." He looked genuinely apologetic. "Val straightened everything out with Talia. She told her I could be a jerk sometimes."

"Just sometimes?" Jack was trying to make his friend squirm.

"Hey, cut me some slack will you. I wasn't tryin' to be a jerk. Me n' Val just got talkin' and she said I made Talia feel outta place when I was complainin' and I need to be more sensitive sometimes."

"Talia's okay now. She thought we were trying to make her feel stupid about the boat that's all. Hey, you and Val seem to be getting along pretty good. What's up with that?"

"Me n' Val always got along good. Where've you been?" Kai's face was flushed.

"Hey, no big deal. You're right. You and Val have been tight for a long time." They climbed aboard *Bad Latitude* as the girls approached. "You ready? Here they come." Jack ended the conversation before any damage could be done. There was no sense spoiling things with his own big mouth.

They paired up for the return ride, with Jack and Talia together at the helm, while Val and Kai shared the seat on the port side of the bow. After retracing their route, they reached the Tolomato River, forty-five minutes from St Augustine. Jack asked Kai to take over the controls.

"Hey Kai, you want to run us in the rest of the way? I need a break." Jack knew Kai could handle the boat and decided it would only help Kai's effort to impress Val. It would also give Jack the chance to relax and talk with Talia for a while, away from the roar of the engine.

Kai took the wheel, doing his best to act as if running *Bad Latitude* was no big deal. As usual, he kept one eye on Val to make sure she was noticing his every move. After a few minutes, she moved to the helm to join him.

"Take it down to St Augustine and we'll tie up at one of the slips at the marina for a while," yelled Jack over the sound of the wind and motor.

Talia gently nudged Jack and pointed toward Kai and Val with her eyes. Val was standing next to Kai, her arm locked into his as he stood behind the wheel. His chest was puffed out and he was the new king of the world.

6

Hot Sauce

Kai docked *Bad Latitude* inside the boat slip with the touch of an expert. In no time, they were tied off and on their way down the gangplank. Jack paid the transient fee to the dock master and told him they would be ashore until later that evening. The attendant made the appropriate notations and attached a bright orange tag to the T-Top rail, which would notify the next attendant that the slip was rented for the remainder of the day.

The two couples ambled along historic St. George Street, stopping at various shops along the way where they picked out tee shirts with pictures of pirates and funny one-liners across the backs. Kai, as a jab aimed at Jack, bought himself a shirt with a huge picture of Bob Marley plastered across the front.

Out of the blue Kai started babbling "Hot sauce! We gotta stop and get some hot sauce!"

Everyone stared at him like he was nuts.

"There's a place around the corner called *Henwee's Hotties.* They sell all kinds of hot sauces with hilarious names and labels. We gotta go before they close," he insisted.

"Why is it called Henwee's?" Val asked.

"The guy went n' burnt all the nerves in the end of his tongue when he was tryin' out all his hot sauces. Now he can't pronounce his R's anymore."

"Really? Is that what happened?" asked Val.

"Weally! No not really. I was jus' makin' that up. Geez, how the heck do I know? What do I look like, a walkin' cyclopedia?"

Everyone laughed at being suckered into the story when Val dropped her own hint in Jack and Talia's direction. "This oughtta be good. We can go check out the hot stuff place and meet up with you guys later if you want."

"I'm tellin' you it's a riot in there. You guys gotta come with us," pressed Kai. Val seemed disappointed.

Talia picked up on the hint, and, knowing that Val was looking for some time with Kai all to herself, made the decision for everyone. "You guys go check out *Henwee's* and we'll meet up with you in front of that old wooden schoolhouse in about an hour."

Kai and Val held hands as they made their way toward Charlotte Street. Jack and Talia continued their walk down St. George Street, stopping when they reached a narrow alleyway with a signpost, reading Treasury Street. Without warning, Jack launched into a pirate tale. It was one of his favorites from one of his earliest storytelling sessions with Pop.

"Nearly three hundred and fifty years ago, on this very street, the pirate Robert Searle, after pillaging the city, was walking toward the wharf as daybreak approached. He turned down here at Treasury Street. A sudden movement caught his eye and he whirled around, blindly firing his pistol, mistakenly thinking he was under attack. To his horror, he found he had shot an innocent little girl. The poor child, orphaned earlier that night during the siege, died instantly. Seeing what he had done, the bloodthirsty pirate was devastated and ravaged with guilt. For two years, he found no peace as he was visited every night by the spirit of his little victim. Night after torturous night she wailed and screamed until daybreak. The continual haunting eventually caused him to lose his mind. One night, finally overtaken by his depression and dove from the stern of his ship, plunging into the swirling depths, trying desperately to end the pain and escape his madness.

Not a trace of Captain Searle was ever found. His shipmates, driven by superstition and fear of bad omens, fought amongst themselves over which course to sail. The disagreement turned into a bloody brawl. There were no survivors. Captain Searle's ship was found two years later, adrift due east from the St. Augustine harbor, overrun with rats crawling across the bleached white bones of the forty three men that died on deck."

Jack concluded the story feigning a look of dread; "St. Augustine is known to be one of the most haunted cities in the entire country. They say there are times on this very street that you will feel a deep chill if you pause at the exact spot where the little girl lost her life. Let's walk down this way and see if we can find it."

"No way am I walking down that street, especially after hearing a story like that," said Talia. "I don't care if it is hocus pocus."

Jack flashed a devilish smile and they continued lazily down the street. "Who says it's hocus pocus?"

They bought ice cream and stopped to listen to a blind man play the guitar, while the man's dog lay on the walkway by his feet, next to an open case being filled with coins and dollar bills. Eventually they were joined in front of the old schoolhouse by Val and Kai, laughing hysterically, carrying bags, and guzzling large bottles of water. Jack supposed they had tried various samples at the hot sauce shop and were now paying the price.

"So whaddya think? Should we take one of those ghost tours now that it's gettin' dark?" suggested Kai hopefully. "They have old fashioned funeral carriages and ghost trains."

"We can take our own ghost tour. We don't need someone else to show us around," said Jack. "My stories are guaranteed to keep you all up for the night."

"If we're taking a vote, I say we do it some other time," Val chimed in. "My tongue's on fire and I just ran out of water. Can't we just chill for a little while."

Talia looked apprehensively toward Jack. "Can you drive the boat in the dark?"

"Sure, that's no problem, but I don't want to get back too late and have my grandparents getting worried. It's probably better if we start for the dock pretty soon."

"So if it ain't the surfer creep," came a raspy twangy voice from behind.

Kai spun on his heels. "Oh, this is great. It just figures that I'd run into you two half wits," he replied defiantly. "I thought you guys'd be in jail by now."

Standing behind Kai and Val were identical twins. Unfortunately, looking alike was definitely not a plus for these two. Both were missing several teeth, and the few that remained were yellowed and rotted. Each had greasy, slimy matted black hair and neither had taken a shower in weeks. They wore sleeveless undershirts with stains and holes and Talia struggled to keep from gagging. The pair reeked of sour sweat mixed with gasoline or paint thinner. Talia supposed it might be thinner since both had paint smeared on the front of their jeans. These two losers were out looking for a fight and Kai was their target.

Jack stepped forward so that his shoulder brushed against his friend. "So Kai, these guys friends of yours?"

"Friends? You gotta be kiddin' me. These guys are brothers, Willie and Billy, an' if you couldn't tell, they're freakin' twins. Believe me, ain't no way we're friends."

"Ya got that right, we ain't yer friends and we're here gonna kick yer rear end all over this here street ya big mouth little punk," growled either Willie or Billy.

"Before you guys start your crap, I've got one question. Is there some reason that you mental giants have the same name? I mean, Willie and Billy are each a nickname for William, so, what's up with that?" asked Jack. He stared at them with a cocky grin.

"He's Wilbur an' ahmm William an' ya kin mahnd yer own binness or we'll be kickin' the crap outta you like we're fixin' to do to him ya moron," threatened Billy.

"Nah, you two dirtballs couldn't kick anyone's butt, especially mine. You're too stupid, and out of shape for that." Jack edged forward in front of Kai.

Talia and Val retreated several steps, both wondering why Jack seemed determined to provoke the pair of dirty creeps. Val worried that the confrontation would escalate into a brawl while Talia was genuinely amused.

"Are you nuts, Rackham? Whaddya tryin' to do, show off or somethin'?" groaned Kai under his breath. "These guys are bad news."

Jack turned toward Kai while watching the twins from the corner of his eye. He had already determined that backing down would be a big mistake, so he remained cocky with his reply, repeating Kai's hushed question for all to hear. "Show off? How would I be showing off? These two are nothing. Besides, I have a weapon and they don't."

"Huh? Weapon? What weapon? You're gonna get us killed."

As Kai's head was twisting back and forth between his friend and the twins, Jack grabbed the bag Kai was holding, reached inside, and yanked out a bottle of hot sauce, just as Willie and Billy lunged. The twins weren't fast enough, and he caught both of them, full in the face, with splashes of fiery hot habanero sauce. Clutching at their burning eyes, they began screaming in agony, giving Jack the opening needed to dump a full dose of the painfully spicy mixture into their wide-open mouths. Willie and Billy dropped to their knees, clawing at their throats and eyes, choking for breath through deep spasms.

"Time to go," yelled Jack and the four took off down a side street, leaving the twins screaming and gasping on all fours in the middle of the old town.

After ten blocks, they slowed to catch their breath. The window shopping and exploring was over for the night and they were on their way to the city pier. Kai kept turning to see if the twins were following. Satisfied that they weren't being chased, he broke the silence.

"You know, that bottle of hot sauce cost me twelve bucks."

Val started giggling. She couldn't believe what she was hearing. Talia was grinning and shaking her head. Jack stopped walking and looked toward Kai with a furious glare. He reached in his pocket and calmly pulled out twelve dollars.

"Maybe I should have left you behind with your hot sauce so those two goons could have pounded the crap out of you."

Kai was surprised at Jack's obvious irritation. "Hey, I don't want your money or nothin'. I really 'preciate you steppin' up for me like that. I was just makin' the comment that the hot sauce cost me twelve bucks."

"Yeah right. Well, next time, I'm going to mind my own business and let you fight your own battles."

Kai was frustrated. "C'mon dude, I didn't really mean anything by it."

Jack decided it was another case of Kai opening his mouth before engaging his brain and backed off. "Okay, we're cool. Come on; let's get to the boat. You know, we're gonna have to keep an eye out for those slimeballs. They're going to be after us now."

"No kiddin'. They've been after me for months and I don't even know why. Musta been somethin' I said," answered Kai matter of factly.

"*NO. NO WAY!* Something *YOU* must've said? I can't even imagine that." Jack was staring incredulously.

The girls were in hysterics watching the two argue back and forth. Kai was trying act like the always-innocent victim while Jack grumbled about Kai's big mouth. Neither of the guys were willing to budge an inch.

They were twenty feet from the boat when Talia heard tires squealing and turned toward the street. A beat up van with ladders racked to the top, screeched across the sidewalk. The twins jumped out and began charging up the pier.

"Boys, we've got company. We gotta go and we gotta go now," Talia calmly announced.

Jack turned to see the twins running toward them up the dock. With two strides, he
was on the deck of *Bad Latitude* reaching for the ignition switch. "Hurry! Get the lines. Let's get outta here!" he hollered.

The engine was fired up and the ropes were off but Jack couldn't throttle forward. There was a large cruiser partially blocking the way and he couldn't risk beating the hulls of the two boats. The situation seemed hopeless.

"Kai, grab the flare gun out of the bag. Maybe that'll scare them off."

"Which bag? You've got a bag for everything on this tug."

"The blue and black one, hurry up, they're getting close."

The girls moved to the starboard side of the bow. Willie and Billy were running like crazed animals. There was pure hatred in their swollen red eyes and they were closing fast. Kai was fumbling inside the bag trying to find the flare gun and wasn't having any luck. The boat was still too close to the dock. Jack was sure the smelly troublemakers could make the jump from the pier to the boat with ease.

Jack started barking orders. "Talia, use the boat hook and push the bow off. I can't open up the throttle until we're clear. Val, push here at the stern. Kai, Where's that flare gun?"

"I'm lookin'. Use some more of that hot sauce!" yelled Kai.

The twins were fifteen feet away. *Bad Latitude* was four feet from the dock and the bow was finally pointing toward open water. It would be close. Talia pushed off with all her strength, but at six feet, the boat pole would reach no further. Val had done her part and there was nothing more that she could do.

"Hit the deck and hold on tight," shouted Jack.

He buried the throttle forward just as the twins leaped into the air, aiming for the stern. Everything seemed to move in slow motion. *Bad Latitude* lurched ahead as Willie's toeless sneaker hit the gunwale by the stern cleat. Billy was in mid air yelling out a hillbilly war cry, his arms flailing in a windmill motion. The engine roared and the bow rose, almost vertically, out of the water. Willie flew backwards away from the boat, Billy wasn't quite so lucky. He had been leaning forward when he started his jump and there was a sickening thump as his forehead hit the starboard rub rail. The escape was complete.

Once safely out of reach, Jack backed off the throttle. The twins were in the water and he watched as they doggie paddled and choked their way toward the dock. Confident that the coast was clear and no one was seriously hurt, he continued toward open water at a no wake speed.

He looked at the girls with a sheepish grin. "I guess they missed the boat."

The girls rolled their eyes and giggled at the weak attempt at humor.

"Awright, here it is. I got it," announced Kai. He stood triumphantly, proudly holding the flare gun above his head.

"My hero," laughed Val.

They wisecracked for the entire ride back to the boathouse. Jack joined in with the jokes, but knew deep down that they had not seen the last of Willie and Billy.

"Geez, I hope they didn't read the boat's name before we got away," said Talia. "They'll be on the lookout for it now."

"Read? You think those idiots can read?" Kai chimed in.

"See. You probably got it all started by saying something just like that," scolded Val.

"Well, at least they finally got a bath." Talia couldn't forget the awful smell.

Val reached in her bag for her cell phone. "All I know is, that's enough excitement for me for one day. I'd better call my Mom so she can pick us up."

"Plenty for me too," sighed Jack, as he tucked *Bad Latitude* into the boatlift.

7

Secret Plans

Kai spent the night at the boathouse, providing Jack the opportunity to ask for Kai's help with his search for the lost gold. The timing was perfect for letting his most trusted friend in on the big secret. It didn't take long for Kai's imagination and enthusiasm to kick into high gear.

"So you're sayin' all we gotta do is find the top of this Indian King's head and the treasure will be buried at the dude's feet?" asked Kai.

"That's the story. Pop already found the skull; we just have to probe around for it during the day, plug it into the GPS once we find it, and go back and dig it up at night so nobody sees us." He knew Kai would want to go over the whole thing at least a dozen times.

"When can we get goin'? I'm good for tomorrow if you want."

"I'm anxious too but Pop wants us to wait until after my parents visit. He doesn't want my mom freaking out about me being in some Indian graveyard at night. In fact, he said to keep my mouth shut about it around Nan too because he doesn't want her all worried," said Jack.

"Nan wouldn't get creeped out about it. She'd probably wanna help," laughed Kai. "Hey, you think the place is haunted don't you?"

"I'm not sure, but Pop thinks it might be. We need to be very careful, just in case. He wants to know what our plan is before we start so he can make sure we're not overlooking anything."

"Yeah, that's just like him, make sure all the bases are covered. You'd think as cautious as he is about stuff, he wouldn't want you to doin' some of the dangerous crap you do," said Kai.

"Well, I don't know yet if it's dangerous. Besides, Pop tells me stories about my dad and uncle when they were younger. They were always getting into all kinds of wild stuff. Nan says they were fearless. Pop says they were just plain nuts, but he always laughs about it."

"Yeah but they weren't diggin' up treasure in a freakin' Injun cemetery in the middle of the night like we're gonna be doin'."

"No, guess you're right about that. All I know is, we're not telling anybody, and that includes my parents, Val, Talia, and anyone else."

"So, you think we could go over there in the morning and check it out a little?" Kai wasn't about to give up without some effort.

Jack let out a tired sigh. "Okay. Let's go over to the state park tomorrow. We can take the tourist boat to Fort Matanzas and scope it out from the top of the lookout tower. We'll bring some binoculars and a camera so we can see where we could anchor up, and take some pictures to use later when we're making our plans. My parents will be here in a couple of days, but they're only staying for a week. When they hit the road, we'll get busy," said Jack.

Grudgingly Kai agreed to let the subject drop. He knew it wasn't an argument he could win. Both were tired. It had been a long day and finally, at three in the morning, they crashed for the night as the third re-run of the day's baseball highlights were repeated on ESPN.

The boys slept until just past noon. Both were starved when they awoke and they hurried from the boathouse toward Nan's kitchen to see what they could scrounge up. Nan was sitting by the pool and nabbed them as they walked past.

"I wondered when you two would come back to life. I suppose you're looking for breakfast, or maybe lunch," said Nan.

"We can find something Nan, there's no need for you to run around taking care of us." Jack was being polite but still hoped she would fix them something.

"Give me ten minutes and you boys can have some breakfast burritos."

Kai perked up. "That sounds great. If you want, I've got some hot sauce."

Nan shook her head as if to warn them. "These will be spicy enough, don't you worry. I'll just mix up some scrambled eggs with some hot sausage, cheddar cheese, red chili peppers, and a few pinches of cayenne. It's already prepared; I just have to throw it all in the skillet. Sound okay to you two?"

"No wonder you visit here so much," said Kai as he turned toward Jack and then back to Nan. "Burritos sound great. Hey Nan, you wouldn't wanna adopt me or somethin' would you? I could stay in the boathouse and keep the cars and boats clean, pull weeds in the gardens, whatever y'all want me to do. You'd get your money's worth."

Nan smiled good-naturedly. "You're already adopted. I've told you plenty of times that Jack doesn't have to be here for you to visit or have dinner with us. You and Pop get along great and he's always looking for someone to take fishing."

The burritos were wolfed down as fast as they hit the plates. Kai managed to put away four while Jack could only handle three. The more they ate the lazier they felt. Nan chuckled as she watched them lean back in their seats rubbing their stomachs like a couple of old men.

"Kai, I hope you're not going to be a stranger when Jack's parents visit. Jack, your other friends are more than welcome to join us anytime as well. I know Val always likes to hang out with us and I'm sure your new friend Talia would like to meet your mom and dad. I'd like to get to know her better myself. She seems like a real nice girl. Maybe she has an older sister for your Uncle Chris." Nan turned her back to the boys so they couldn't see her smile. Fixing up Jack's uncle seemed to be Nan's mission in life. So far, she'd had little success as a matchmaker.

Kai picked up on Nan's interest in Talia immediately. He looked over at Jack and started making exaggerated kissing gestures. Jack wasn't amused and quickly changed the subject.

"I'm not sure what everyone's doing Nan. I think she and Val have plans most of the week so I doubt if either of them will be around much. We're gonna be busy getting ready for the holiday anyway, and dad and Uncle Chris want to do some fishing with me n' Pop while they're here." He gave Kai the *knock it off and shut up* look.

"Well, that's fine. The invitation is always open. Don't worry about asking before bringing any of your friends around," she said.

Kai and Jack each gave Nan big hugs, thanked her for making breakfast, and returned to the boathouse to get changed. Kai borrowed some clothes, with the promise that he would return them washed and folded. Jack knew he would never see them again.

They took the Jet Skis to the park across from Fort Matanzas. Jack carried a pair of binoculars and a waterproof digital camera. The tour boat left the Ranger station every hour up until four-thirty each day giving them plenty of time to make the trip. The dock at the fort was off limits to any vessels other than the Ranger's huge pontoon boat. Jack read a poster describing the fort's history as a boatload of visitors were discharging to the exit platform.

During the early eighteenth century, St. Augustine was defended against direct attacks from the sea by the massive fortress, *Castillo de San Marcos*. There was, however, no protection from invaders planning entrance to the city using the Matanzas River from the south. Construction of Fort Matanzas was completed in 1742. Coquina, a local shell stone, held together with a mortar mixture made from oyster shells, was used to build the armed outpost. As work on the battle station was nearing completion, the British, believing that the waterway provided perfect access for an ambush on the city, sailed into the river. Spanish cannons drove the intruders off and the British abandoned the attack. It was the only time in history that the guns of the old outpost were ever fired in battle.

Jack and Kai boarded the tourist boat and remained quiet for the short ride to the small fortress. They waited to exit the boat until the visitors had made their way across the floating dock. The boys bypassed the assembly of sightseers clustered around the tour guide, who was dressed in the uniform of a Spanish soldier from that period, busily narrating the history of the old garrison. After walking across the cannon deck and into the soldier's quarters, filled with replica furnishings, they climbed the ladder to the observation tower and immediately headed to the west end of the platform and scanned the grassy area known as Rattlesnake Island. After a few minutes, they picked out the location where three waterways converged and Jack began snapping pictures.

"I've seen enough, how about you? We'll get started next week. Maybe we should take the kayaks and pretend to be nature freaks. It's probably shelly and muddy over there anyway and I don't want to tear up the boat. Think you can paddle that far?" asked Jack.

"Yeah, that's no problem. I haven't kayaked in a long time, probably since last summer with you, but I've been surfing most every day since spring so I'm in good shape." Kai's face brightened. "Hey, why don't we give it a try today?"

"We can buzz nearby on the way back on the Jet Skis but it's almost low tide. I doubt if we could get close enough to anchor and walk around. Besides, we're only wearing flip flops and they don't call it Rattlesnake Island for nothing."

"Good point. You 'specially hafta lookout for those pygmy rattlers. Those little buggers can do some damage and you can't see 'em 'til it's too late," said Kai.

As Jack suspected, there were too many shell banks in the way to get very close without risking disaster. Pop was cool about letting him use the Jet Skis but wouldn't cut him any slack if he did something stupid on the water. Taking the machines too close to shore and tearing up the bottoms would certainly qualify as something stupid. After their trip to the west side of the island, where Jack snapped another dozen pictures, they raced each other back to dock and put the Jet Skis away. Using Pop's computer Jack downloaded the pictures and printed out the best shots. Back at the boathouse, they pulled out the charts of the waterway, which showed the entire island. The charts contained specific warnings about the shell beds and depth limits and several danger markers were highlighted. Jack decided to ask Pop what he thought they should do about getting through the shallows to survey the area.

"Pop, we went over to the old fort to check out the island. We've looked over the charts but I'm not sure how we could get close enough with the boat, especially running over there at night. What do you think we should do?" he asked.

"Your best bet is to check out the tides and map the route with a GPS. I like your idea about using kayaks during the day. I could probably rig up a battery and depth finder to one of 'em so you can keep track, those charts aren't always accurate. It might take a few trips to plot the course. When I was over there, it was during high tide and I was in a little flat bottom skiff. Your boat draws a lot more water, so you're right to be concerned. I'm impressed that you two recognized the depth problem right away. I was sure that that was gonna be the first thing I'd have to point out." Pop never bothered to look up as he sat on a chair busily shucking corn.

"How the heck do you hook up a depth finder to a kayak?" asked Kai.

Pop paused, staring at Kai with a *how dare you question me* expression on his face. "You let me worry about that. In the meantime, we've got company comin' so let's put all of this on hold 'til everyone's gone. No need to go stirrin' up a hornet's nest." The truth was, Pop wasn't sure how he would hook up a depth finder, but wasn't about to admit it to Kai.

Kai was invited for dinner, as he had hoped he would be. After he left, Jack hung out to visit with Nan and Pop. He would have to help out as they prepared for his parent's visit. Once again, Nan insisted that he invite Talia, Val, and Kai to stop by after the family arrived. At ten o'clock, he reluctantly made the phone calls.

Talia was giddy. It had been a great day. Her dad had called to tell her they were moving from California, giving her an extra couple of weeks to spend with her new friends. Jack's invitation to meet the rest of his family was an unexpected bonus. She called Val to see if she wanted to go with her to shop for some new clothes. Maybe they would get their nails done.

Over and over, Val assured Talia that everything would be perfectly cool, giggling at her uncharacteristic enthusiasm and non-stop babbling. Finally, Val gave up and broke the connection, leaving Talia chattering away to an empty phone.

8

Rattlesnake Island

"Christine you look wonderful," said Nan as she hugged
her daughter in law. "It's been forever since we've all been
together."

"Nan, I'm finally here," Isabel called out as she pranced
through the front door.

After all, of the hugs and kisses were taken care of,
everyone hurried outside to the pool. In no time at all, Jack's
family was relaxing in the crystal clear water. Pop made himself
useful, taking turns between the stainless steel barbecue grill
and the tiki bar. Isabel's first choice was one of Pop's famous
Pina Coladas, minus the rum. Never one to be far from her
mother, she waded across the pool where her mom and Nan
were busy catching up on gossip and fine-tuning plans for the
visit ahead.

It didn't take long for the girls to settle on a trip to Sea World. They would spend a couple of days in Orlando while the guys went fishing. In the meantime, Jack's dad was on the phone trying to track down his brother Chris.

"Mike, what makes you think anything's changed with that brother of yours. He won't be here 'til tomorrow mornin'," laughed Pop.

"He said he might make it this afternoon," replied Jack's dad with a straight face.

"Yeah right, and I'm gonna pitch for the New York Yankees next week."

As usual, Uncle Chris made his grand entrance late the next morning.

The weather was terrific for the entire week and time passed by quickly. Nan and Pop went overboard making sure everyone had everything they could possibly want. Isabel got her wish and swam with the dolphins at Sea World and Jack fished his dad, and uncle on *Laffin' Gaff*. The guys also played several rounds of golf at *Sawgrass*, home of the TPC pro golf tournament in nearby Ponte Vedra. The days at the beach were a blast. Toward the end of the week, Jack's mom and dad took the deck boat out for a day all to themselves.

Kai, Val, and Talia hung out as much as possible. They were made to feel like they belonged, and pitched in to help with the chores wherever they could. By week's end, Isabel had adopted Talia as her new big sister. When it was time for Jack's family to leave, a tearful Isabel made her promise to stay in touch by phone and email.

The treasure hunt started the next morning. The boys packed their gear into waterproof backpacks. Included was a hand held GPS, a couple of folding shovels, a portable marine radio, a small first aid kit, some water bottles, gloves, and two pair of knee high rubber boots. They would slide the boots on as soon as they landed on the island for protection against the poisonous snakes they were bound to run across. Jack had also stashed a copy of the map inside the bag.

As Pop had promised, a depth finder was mounted to one of the kayaks. He warned them to take it easy dragging the kayak onto shore so that the sensor on the bottom wouldn't be snapped off. Pop let Kai think the rig was a work of genius, not letting on that he had actually paid a mechanic at the marina to install it.

Kai took the lead as they shoved off from the dock. It was early morning, the water was calm, and the temperature was approaching the mid eighties. They had been paddling for half an hour when Jack started charting the water with the depth finder and GPS. A quarter mile from their landing point, their arms and shoulders began tiring.

Reaching the shoreline, they stepped from the kayaks and dragged them ashore, hiding them behind the high grass. After pulling on their rubber boots, Jack grabbed the map, probe, and GPS, while Kai carried the folding shovels and water bottles. Following the map, they marched east for eight hundred yards, mapping their progress on the GPS screen. Working the area closely matching the old map, they made up a grid with stick markers spaced every four feet. They probed and dug shallow holes within the grid for a few hours. The temperature stood at ninety-seven degrees when the boys began their exhausting paddle home.

For the next five days, Jack and Kai continued their quest with no results and each day they returned to the boathouse dog-tired. Pop encouraged them after every trip, reminding them that the potential reward could make all of the hard work worthwhile. He finally suggested they take a day off to relax, clear their heads, and get a well-deserved break. Kai thought the idea made plenty of sense but Jack wanted to push on. Sunday turned out to be blustery. Not wanting to paddle against the stiff winds, the boys put their search on hold for the day, taking advantage of conditions perfect for kite boarding.

Jack and Kai arrived at the Matanzas inlet just before ten where they found the sky filled with huge billowing kites. Boarders strapped in harnesses attached to the kites by nylon lines, were being pulled across the surface of the waves. The boys slipped into their harnesses and carefully stretched and separated the lines to avoid tangles. Leaning back to allow the wind to fill the kites, they struggled against the cross breezes into the water, secured their feet in the boards and began riding the wind. Kai was a local expert, doing acrobatic jumps, twists, and flips in the breakers. He called it *getting big air*. Jack was a novice, but held his own with speed and agility. The beach was crammed with onlookers and cameras were clicking away, all pointed toward the daredevils in the surf.

Another week of digging followed and Kai's patience was wearing thin. He didn't want to let Jack down, but his summer was nearing an end. They had been digging for ten days, five straight since their day at the beach. Now thinking it was a lost cause, he was trying to convince Jack to back off, at least for a few days. Kai would keep up his end of the bargain but he desperately needed a long break from what he called grave digging very soon.

The heat was building again. Jack was shoveling and probing, worried that maybe they hadn't been digging deep enough all along. Kai was busy putting the grasses back in place, so evidence of their exploration would be disguised. As the sweat poured down Jack's face, he stopped to dry off and catch his breath. He reached into his back pocket and removed a handkerchief that Pop had given him as a joke. It had the Rackham skull and crossed cutlasses on it. He smiled, and tied it on as a bandanna, hoping it might help change their luck.

He knew Kai was getting bored, tired, and frustrated and it was only a matter of time before his friend would want to quit the search. There was no way he could blame him. If Kai wanted to drop out, he would continue on his own. For Jack, finding the gold had become an obsession.

It didn't take long for the lucky rag to work its magic. There was an unusual hollow scraping sound as the shovel burrowed through the soft moist earth. Jack looked over to see if Kai had noticed. He hadn't. Carefully, Jack began poking and shoveling small loads of dirt. Within minutes, there appeared a yellow rounded shell. Doing his best to shield Kai from seeing what he was doing, he turned with his back facing his friend. He would never hear the end of it if it turned out to be a false alarm. Continuing on, he dug a circle around the bone-like piece. Finally, positive that he had uncovered a skull, he let Kai in on his discovery.

"Hey Kai, you ever see a shell like this?"

"You want shells? Go to the beach. I'm sweatin' my rear end off and you're huntin' for shells. Don't go diggin' any more. I wanna take a break n' do some surfin' or somethin'," barked a cranky Kai as he tossed an armload of smelly marsh grass to the ground disgustedly.

"Okay, no big deal, we can quit. I just thought this one looked kinda like an old skull."

Kai stared at him. If this was a joke, he wasn't in the mood. Every muscle in his body ached. He was sweaty, itchy, and dreading another long paddle up river before he could rest. "If you're jerkin' my chain, I'm tellin' you I'm walkin' right over to that kayak and you can dig to China for all I care. I'm workin' like a landscaper, 'cept without gettin' paid."

"Well, take a look for yourself and tell me what *you* think this is," said Jack.

For Kai, a truly foul mood was a rarity and Jack rightly concluded that his friend had reached the breaking point. It was definitely a skull, and it was in the vicinity shown on the map. He could only hope the skeleton was still attached, and that the gold was buried at the bottom of the grave as the diary promised.

Kai stomped over to the shallow hole and squinted as he stared down at the shell-like object. Very slowly, he wiped the sweat from his eyes, as if it was distorting his vision. Finally, he turned and peered at Jack, the trace of a smile starting to form. "You think this is it?"

"Well, we need to dig some more and find out."

Kai was suddenly full of energy. "Let's get busy then."

"Maybe we should wait until dark. We can't afford to have someone notice us working in some big hole out here in the open."

"Are you nuts? We gotta find out if this is really the place."

Jack pretended to give in reluctantly. "Alright, I'm going to dig where the ribs should be and see if there's a skeleton attached. You want to start digging about four or five feet away from the head? The diary says the gold is buried by the feet. We're going to have to keep the holes and piles small so nobody sees we're up to something."

It didn't take long to confirm. The bones were intact. After entering the exact coordinates into the GPS, Jack backfilled his part of the hole and moved over to help Kai dig where they thought the feet should be. Nearly seven feet below the surface, Kai hit something solid. After carefully clearing the loose soils away, they located the top of an ancient battered box. The temptation to keep going was unbearable, but digging it up the rest of the way during daylight was impossible. There was no way to bring the box up and haul it back to the house in the kayaks. The final dig would have to wait.

The boys disguised the work area, spreading marsh grass over the newly filled hole. They were exhausted, sweaty, and grimy but, between the two of them, couldn't have felt better. Dragging themselves back to the kayaks, neither could keep from smiling, and both ignored the screaming protests of their tired, aching muscles as they paddled up river. Jack couldn't wait to tell Pop.

Thoroughly exhausted, they finally reached their destination, and crawled from the kayaks to the dock and limped to the boathouse. Good news or not, walking into the house as filthy as they were, was not an option. Half an hour later, Kai and Jack, now showered and changed, were on their way to the main house to share their exciting news with Pop.

Kai stopped dead, stretching his aching arms above his head as he stared at *Bad Latitude*. "We're idiots."

"What are you talking about?" asked Jack.

"All this time we coulda been towin' the kayaks with your boat, anchored it up in deep water near the island, and kayaked to shore," answered Kai.

Jack looked from Kai to the *Bad Latitude* and back to Kai. "You're right. We're idiots."

Kai couldn't believe Jack was admitting to such an obvious miscalculation so easily. "Really? You didn't think of that before?"

"I thought of it. An empty boat anchored right next the channel would have worked like a billboard. It would have stirred up plenty of suspicion and we'd have had company."

"Okay. Guess you're right. That's good. I feel better now."

They walked in through the back door where Nan was busy arranging flowers in a crystal vase.

"Hi Nan. Hey that looks nice," said Jack.

"Since when did you ever notice a flower arrangement Jackson?" Nan's radar kicked into high gear, immediately sensing something was up.

"Really Nan, the flowers look great," Kai added.

"What's wrong? If you guys have gotten yourselves into some kind of hot water, you'd better come clean right away." Nan eyed them both suspiciously.

"Everything's fine. No problem. Really," laughed Jack nervously.

"I'm telling you two, something's going on. Don't forget, I had boys of my own, and they didn't get away with very much. Don't think you two will either." Nan wasn't smiling now.

"Really, everything's fine. We were kinda' hopin' we could grab somethin' to eat so we were butterin' you up," said Kai. He was good at thinking on his feet.

"Alright, I'll fix you boys something, but I'd better not hear that you two have been up to no good," said Nan as she walked to the kitchen.

Jack let out a light sigh of relief. "So where's Pop?"

"Oh, he and his buddy Matt went to Tampa to watch the Yankees play the Rays. He won't be home until late tonight," said Nan as she rooted through the refrigerator.

Jack's shoulders sagged. His big news would have to wait. "That's cool. I hope his Yankees win."

The St. Augustine Lighthouse

9

Dead Girls

Talia's phone rang. She checked the caller I D and let the call go to voice mail. It was Jack. Why should she answer the phone? Both girls had been practically ignored by the guys for much of the past two weeks and all that was offered as an excuse was, they were *busy*. Let him keep leaving messages.

"So what are the big plans for tonight?" asked Val, with just a dash of sarcasm. If it had been her phone ringing, she would have answered. She wasn't into playing games. Kai had apologized the day before for being scarce and said they would get together in a day or two. Val asked what was going on, but all she could get out of him was that he and Jack were working on something, that for the time being, had to be kept secret. He couldn't go into any details, he said, because he didn't want to jinx it. Jack hadn't offered even that much of an explanation.

Talia was in a snippy mood. "I don't know. Maybe we should just hang out here tonight."

That was all Val needed to hear. "Well, you go ahead and hang out. I'm going home. I'll text Kai and see if he has any plans. Then I'll make up my mind about what to do. If Kai's busy, I'll see if Nina wants to go out. What I'm *not* going to do is sit around here and mope." Val angrily grabbed her stuff from the chair and stomped toward the door.

Talia was caught completely off guard. "Why are you ticked off at me?"

"First of all," replied Val, "my summer is over in a few weeks and I'm not wasting what's left of it sitting around here. Secondly, they don't *have* to spend time with us. You're acting like everybody owes *you* attention and your attitude stinks. How many voice mails and text messages has Jack left you anyway?" Val didn't wait for an answer as she banged through the door, assuming, as she left, that her friendship with Talia was probably over.

Talia didn't give chase. She was fuming and gathered her things and padded toward the shower. Who was Val to jump all over her anyway? Who did she think she was? A little later, as she finished blow-drying her hair it occurred to her that maybe Val had a point. Jack had left at least six messages and she had not returned a single one. As much as she hated to admit it, he wasn't her boyfriend and he didn't owe her a thing. Swallowing her pride, she grabbed the phone.

"Hello?"

"Hi Val, it's me."

"Yeah, I know. We have caller I D like everyone else. What's up?" Val was defensive, expecting an argument.

Talia got to the point. "I wanted to apologize. You're right. I've been acting like a jerk. I'm going to call Jack when I hang up. Maybe the four of us could get together and do something tonight."

Val reverted to her old self instantly. "Your apology is accepted and yes, I'm all about doing something tonight. See what he has to say and let me know. If they're busy, we can meet up and go downtown and do whatever you want."

Val's phone rang as soon as she had hung up. This time it was Kai.

"Hey Val, whaddya up to?"

"Nothing really, I was waiting for Talia to see what she wants to do tonight. Got any suggestions?"

"Yeah, actually Jack was tryin' to get hold of you guys to see if you wanted to go to the lighthouse tonight."

"The lighthouse closes at six. You can't get in there at night."

"Jack's Pop is a member of some association that takes care of the place. He has a friend working there who said it would be okay, as long as he had some notice. You know how Jack likes all that spooky stuff."

"Sounds cool. Talia's probably on the phone with him right now. I'm definitely up for it," said Val. She couldn't wait to see him and didn't try to hide her enthusiasm. The truth was, she would be happy watching a bunch of old ladies play bingo as long as she was with Kai. Hanging up, she rushed around to get ready. This would be a blast. Being in the lighthouse at night was something most people never experienced.

Nan dropped the boys off near the boat ramp across from the lighthouse at eight-thirty. Kai was looking forward to seeing Val again. Jack was only interested in exploring the lighthouse. The fact was, Kai had badgered him into calling Talia the last few times.

The girls arrived and, as part of a planned move, hugged the guys tightly. Kai was all smiles. Jack was less enthused but went along with the greeting without complaint. They walked across the street to the lighthouse park and knocked on the door of the keeper's house. A man wearing stained khakis and a wrinkled denim shirt answered the door.

"Can I help you?"

"Uh, Mr. Farrell? My grandfather told me you would be expecting us." Jack felt like an intruder. There was little doubt that they had interrupted Mr. Farrell's evening nap.

"Ah! You must be young Jack Rackham." The man smiled. "Searching for some adventure I suppose."

"Well, I've been here plenty of times during the day but Pop says there's nothing like this place at night. He says the lighthouse is haunted."

"Indeed it is. Indeed it is. Come in and I'll give you a little history before you start to explore. You can introduce me to your friends here as well," said Mr. Farrell. He turned and shuffled into the hundred-year-old house.

They entered a large room with a collection of antique furnishings and each found a seat. Mr. Farrell, after retrieving a thick scrapbook, made himself comfortable in a high backed chair, stretching his feet out to rest on a tired looking ottoman. Jack introduced everyone and Mr. Farrell proceeded to explain the history of the lighthouse. The book contained a fascinating collection of old pictures, letters, and newspaper clippings. Several of them were removed and carefully passed around as the story was told.

"The first lighthouse was actually a wooden tower built sometime between 1565 and 1586. It was burnt down in 1586, along with most of the city of St. Augustine, by the English pirate Sir Francis Drake. Nearly one hundred years later, 1683 to be exact, the Spanish built a new tower using coquina, the same material used for *Castillo de San Marcos*. Over the years, many renovations and additions were completed and several buildings added, making it more of a complex than a simple tower."

"Soon after Florida became a U.S. territory, the lookout tower was converted to a lighthouse. At that point, a full time light keeper was needed. A fellow by the name of Juan Andreu was hired to keep the light fueled and operational while maintaining the buildings and grounds. It was in 1859 when the first documented tragedy occurred, as Mr. Andreu's cousin fell from the tower and was killed. There was actually talk at the time that it may not have been an accident."

Kai leaned closer. "Is he one of the ghosts hauntin' the place?"

"No, I doubt it, but I'll get to that shortly. You see, this is a different lighthouse and it's in a new location. As the sea continued to take back more land, it was decided that a new complex should be built further inland. The new lighthouse, the one you see today, was completed in 1874. Over one million bricks were used, making the tower rise up to one hundred and sixty five feet. There are two hundred and nineteen steps from the bottom to the tower platform above. Six years after the new lighthouse was made operational, the old tower, as predicted, collapsed into the sea."

Kai interrupted again. "What about the ghosts?"

"Patience lad, patience. I'm getting to that." Mr. Farrell continued the story. "It was during construction of the new lighthouse that the second known tragedy struck. Three teenagers, all girls, were tragically run over by a rail cart used for hauling construction materials from the beach on a temporary steel track. It was the type you've probably seen used in stories of old coal mines. Two of the girls were the daughters

74

of the construction superintendent, Hezekia Pittee. Now it is said that the teenagers continue to roam the grounds searching for their parents. They get very agitated, going to great lengths to frighten our guests. The young spirits are most active as dusk approaches and seem curiously attracted to people of about your age. I should also mention that sometimes and somehow, the old construction superintendent visits. I say somehow because he died years later at his home in Maine, yet manages to appear somewhat regularly. Apparently, he has a mean streak, a bitter spirit is the term, and must be trying to find or protect his children. I've been told that he suffered tremendous guilt over their deaths, and never recovered from his heartbreak. His spirit is the one to watch out for. I have not seen him myself but I've heard many breathtaking accounts shared with me by folks that I know to be truthful and very down to earth."

"Geez. You think we'll bump into that guy tonight?" asked Kai.

"If I may be blunt, I certainly hope not. As I said, he is known to be an angry, maybe even an evil spirit. It would be very wise for all of you to stick together as you climb the tower. By the way, when you get to the top, hold onto the railing for good measure," warned Mr. Farrell. He took on an ominous tone, trying not to chuckle. The wide-eyed teenaged stares were proof that he hadn't lost his ability to tell a chilling tale. "If, by chance, you encounter old Hezekia Pittee, return here immediately. Don't try playing ghost chaser. I would hate to see any of you returning to haunt these grounds." He allowed himself a slight smile and dramatic stare. "Now, you all better get started, it's getting late and it would be rather rude to make our spirits wait."

Mr. Farrell walked with them to the base of the lighthouse and unlocked the door. As they waited, Jack noticed that a thick fog had settled in around the grounds, adding to the eerie feeling of dread already creeping up on him. He couldn't understand it. Scary stories and old dark places had never bothered him in the past. There was something supernatural about the place. Once inside he knew something terrible was about to happen. He could feel it, but kept quiet.

It didn't take long. By the time they reached the fourth landing, they were hearing strange noises. First was the sound of footsteps on the concrete floor below, followed by light rhythmic breathing directly ahead on the stairs. The group continued upward on the spiraling iron treads toward the tower deck. At the next landing, the air became very cold and damp. Val was the first to hang back.

"S-S-Something's up here," she whispered.

"I hear stuff too but haven't seen anything. It's okay. Let's keep moving. We just gotta stay together." Kai was attempting to sound brave and reassuring. He reached for Val's hand and they continued on.

Talia let out a short panicked scream while pointing toward the wall to Kai's left. Blood was oozing through the painted brick. Kai jumped at the sound of her scream, rubbing his shoulder and arm against the sticky black red fluid clotting its way downward to the floor below. He grabbed for the rail, fighting his own urge to yell out.

The lights went out. They had reached the last landing before the top platform and now found themselves plunged into a blackness that none had experienced before. Everyone froze. The approaching sound of light whispers and laughter could be heard from behind and above. As they turned toward the sound, the door to the platform creaked opened. Moonlight peeked into the stair tower from above, illuminating two distinct shapes rising up from behind the terrified foursome. Talia and Val moved behind the boys edging their way backwards toward the top of the stair tower. Val was shaking uncontrollably, never taking her eyes off of the apparitions forming and circling below.

Jack reached for the camera he had stuffed into his back pocket, tapped the button to turn the power on, and felt the lens extend. The spirits were now only half a dozen steps away. He was facing a once in a lifetime chance to capture a picture of real ghosts. If he ran away, the opportunity would be lost. He raised the camera very deliberately aligning it carefully to center the pair of dead visitors. There was a slight pause in their forward motion and he quickly snapped the picture. As the flash went off, the high pitched, ear-piercing screaming started.

Val was the first to reach the observation platform with Talia pushing her from behind. She turned as Kai dove through the doorway expecting to see Jack on his heels. Several seconds passed and there was no sign of him.

"Hold hands and wrap your arms around this railing," yelled Kai. "I gotta go back."

Kai rushed inside, hopped down three steps and fell backwards hard against the stair treads. The spirit shapes could be distinguished in startling detail and he found himself staring upward at the two girls described by Mr. Farrell, the ones that had died in the accident so long ago. Their tragic deaths had left them hideously disfigured and their grotesque features caused Kai to gasp in horror.

Jack was surrounded, suspended above the stairs, being carried slowly toward the top of the lighthouse by the spirits. He was motionless; chin pointed downward touching his chest, eyes closed. There was no sign of life. The camera, still in his right hand, continued flashing at five second intervals. The bright flashes added a frightening strobe effect to the horrible scene. Kai had never known such raw fear. Fighting against the temptation to escape and save himself, he gathered his courage and leaped into the air, desperately reaching to grab onto Jack's ankle, trying to keep his best friend from being carried away into the world of the dead.

10

Hezekia Pittee

Pop felt uneasy. The Yankees had won the game in a yawner and he was on his way home. Something was up. He called the house. Nan answered on the first ring, a bad sign.

"Hi. Just called to see how everything was goin' and let you know I'm about an hour or so away." Pop was trying to act casual and unconcerned. When Nan went quiet for an extra moment, he knew there was a problem.

"Jack hasn't called yet for me to pick them up, and doesn't answer his phone," said Nan as calmly as she could manage. "I dropped them off at the island to meet the girls. He said he would call before it got too late. I'm worried that something's gone wrong."

"Okay, relax honey," said Pop. He tried sounding confident without feeling it. "Weren't they meeting up with John Farrell to tour the lighthouse?"

"That's what they said. I can't believe they would run off somewhere else without at least checking in."

"I'm gonna call Farrell right now and see if they're still there. You know how John likes to tell his stories and show all those pictures. I'll call you right back."

It took twelve rings before Pop had Mr. Farrell on the line. "John, I'm sorry to be callin' so late but Deb and I are tryin' to track down Jack and his friends. She said they were goin' over to walk through the lighthouse but hasn't heard anything from them since droppin' 'em off. They're usually pretty good about callin' and keepin' us in the loop."

"Well, I fell asleep here waiting for them to come down from the tower. Maybe they all decided to wander toward town," said Mr. Farrell as he tried to stifle a yawn.

"John, I think they would have at least stopped to thank you for lettin' them explore the place. I assume you had that scrapbook of yours out."

"Oh we had a fine time talking about the history and the light keepers and some of the ghost stories and such…"

"John, hold on a minute. How long were you storytellin'?"

"I'd guess it must have been well over an hour, hour and a half maybe."

"Awright, I'm on my way back from Tampa, about an hour away. I need you to please go inside the lighthouse and check things out. Maybe they're still runnin' around and maybe they left. I just need to find out so we can make sure everything's okay. Deb's really worried."

"No problem, I'll take a walk over there right now and call you back." Mr. Farrell sounded concerned as he finally noticed the time.

Walking outside into the damp fog, Mr. Farrell noticed that the lights in the utility building at the base of the tower were out. Gazing upward toward the top, a chill ran through his body. Anxiety took hold, causing him to experience shortness of breath. The light from the Fresnel lens, always bright white, was blood red and turning at half speed. The panic was overwhelming. He needed to check on his young visitors and thought about calling for help. Worried that everyone would think he had gone over the edge, perhaps believing his own tales of paranormal events, he proceeded alone. Grabbing a sturdy flashlight, he walked hesitantly toward the tower. Reaching for the door, he found it slightly ajar. Taking a deep breath, he entered the lighthouse with an overwhelming sense of dread.

Pop called Nan and described his brief conversation with Mr. Farrell, adding that he would make a detour to the lighthouse on the way home. Explaining that he was sure the storytelling took longer than Mr. Farrell had recalled, he assured her all was fine and that he suspected the kids were just caught up with having fun exploring the tower and lost track of time. Pop also reminded Nan that cell phones did not get good reception on the island. It would take him less than an hour to get there but expected to hear back from John shortly. Hanging up, he accelerated, trying to cut his travel time by half.

Once inside the tower, Mr. Farrell heard the sounds of screaming from above while noticing the unmistakable scent of pipe tobacco. People who claimed to have seen the ghost of

Hezekia Pittee always started their story with a description of the not so sweet smell of a pipe. His hand trembled as he aimed the flashlight toward the darkened circular stairway to begin the long climb. Beyond the first landing, he found his path blocked by a spirit with a long ratty white beard, dressed in old-fashioned overalls and large brimmed straw hat. It was smoking a pipe. Not sure if what he was seeing was real, Mr. Farrell blinked his eyes several times. The ghoul was still there. As he shined the flashlight toward the face, the image glided toward him with outstretched hands. Terrified, Mr. Farrell began backpedaling down the twisting iron stairs. His flashlight beam found the phantom's face. The bearded spirit had no eyes. Mr. Farrell turned to run but lost his balance, tumbling head first down the curved iron treads. He was unconscious before the flashlight shattered against the concrete below.

Nan couldn't sit by and wait any longer. She grabbed her keys and ran through the door. The Escalade screeched from the brick driveway onto the blacktop, barely pausing for oncoming traffic. Cruising along A1A at double the speed limit, she gave no thought to being stopped by the Sheriff's Department. That was the least of her worries. It had been fifteen minutes since she had talked to Jack's Pop and knew by his tone that he was concerned. Pulling into the parking lot in front of the lighthouse, Nan skidded to a stop, inches from the picket fence that ran between the keeper's house and the visitor's center. She left the vehicle running with the lights burning and driver's door wide open.

Rushing into the darkened tower, she switched her phone to the flashlight accessory. It didn't provide much light but was better than nothing. She started up the spiraling steel stairs, taking them two at a time. The sounds from above echoed throughout the chamber. The mix of wails and screams gave her a start but she continued upward, her heart pounding.

Just beyond the first landing, she stumbled headlong over something on the steps. Nan let out a yell as her shoulder rammed hard against the iron railing. With the tiny light from the phone, she could see Mr. Farrell sprawled across the steps. He was breathing but his head was bloody from a jagged gash. She would have to tend to him later. Ignoring the sharp pain in her shoulder, she resumed the climb. At the seventh landing a green glow of light appeared and a bearded eyeless specter wearing a straw hat blocked her way. Looking past the ghost, Nan could see her grandson suspended high above the stairs between a pair of floating spirits, and Kai, just below, holding onto Jack's ankle with both hands. The girls were at the top of the staircase screaming hysterically.

Getting past the bearded visitor from beyond was her first challenge and she continued climbing. At first, the ghost retreated, its movement barely perceptible. Then it smiled, taking on a look of menacing evil while holding out its bony hand. Nan knew that backing down would be a costly mistake. She had to get to Jack quickly and to do that, she couldn't show any fear.

"Get out of my way. You can't stop me!" Nan hollered.

A blood-curdling scream, like nothing she had heard in her life, erupted from the bearded spirit, but Nan continued forward with determined strides. The ghost inched toward her with both claw like hands extended, but she never paused, staring unafraid into the eyeless sockets.

"I said, get out of my way. Scream all you want. I'm not afraid of you. You're dead you pitiful, miserable old creep. Get in your grave and leave us alone."

Suddenly, what appeared as flesh on the ghost's hands and face began to ripple and spasm, turning several shades of green, yellow, and brown. Worms and maggots squirmed in and out of the eye sockets and nostrils, while others pierced the rotted skin at the throat. Within seconds, bone became visible and the clothing began to sag. As she crossed the step guarded by Hezekia Pittee, the spirit collapsed, unable to prevent Nan from moving past. Dust filtered through the iron grating to the floor several stories below. The last trace of Hezekia Pittee would be erased by a broom, pushed by a maintenance worker early the very next morning.

Approaching the upper tier of the staircase, she could see the two spirits trying to pull Jack upward toward the roof. Kai was still holding onto him with both hands clamped like the jaws of a pit bull. He wasn't letting go. The creatures were screaming and howling wildly. Jack was totally unresponsive.

Very calmly but firmly Nan called out, "Jackson! Jackson! You get down here right now. I won't tell you again."

Jack's eyes fluttered and the camera dropped from his hand, clanking onto the landing behind Kai. Slowly his body moved downward as the spirits continued to hiss and scream.

"Come on Jack. They want to take you somewhere that Pop and I don't want you to go. Come down here with your friends and me so we all can go home. Hurry now. Pop is on his way," said Nan. She gave the order in a gentle, controlled tone.

Jack was awake and began working himself fee, unaware that he was being held precariously in place above the very long set of curving stairs. He would never survive a fall from that height.

"Pull down as hard as you can for just a couple more minutes Kai," Nan instructed calmly. She positioned herself to the opposite side in order to break Jack's fall in case the spirits suddenly let go. Nan noticed that Kai had tucked both of his feet below the underside of the steel treads and wondered admiringly how long he had maintained his grip.

When he was within reach, Nan took his hand and guided him down the rest of the way. Once Jack was loose, Kai collapsed onto the landing shaking and exhausted.

Jack's skin felt icy cold. His arms and wrists would be badly bruised. The girls tearfully rushed to the sides of the boys. As they did, Nan stood to face the dead daughters of Hezekia Pittee.

"You can join your father now. He has left this world forever. Maybe he's finally at peace. There's nothing left for you here anymore. Go rest," whispered Nan very gently.

The raging spirits were transformed before everyone's eyes. Calmness settled over them and their faces reverted to the glowing beauty that each spirit enjoyed before the tragic accident. Smiling peacefully, they faded away. As they disappeared, the lights blinked on.

Seconds later, everyone jumped, startled by a loud crash from the bottom of the tower. Pop's voice echoed from below. They yelled from above that everyone was safe and started the long climb down the staircase.

They stopped at the first landing where Pop was leaning over his good friend Mr. Farrell. To Pop it seemed he'd had an accident trying to climb the tower. Nan figured it differently, supposing that Mr. Farrell was the victim of a very brief encounter with Hezekia Pittee. Pop placed a call to nine-one-one and waited for an emergency vehicle to arrive as Nan and the kids exited into the dense fog outside.

Nan obeyed the speed limit, driving in silence back to the house. Talia and Val called their families to let them know everything was okay. They explained that there had been a minor mishap and had been stuck in the lighthouse. Being as late as it was, all agreed it would be best for the girls to stay over. Once back at the house, they sat around the great room drinking iced tea and piecing every part of the story together.

Pop arrived an hour later. He was upset about his friend, and sat down heavily in his favorite chair. After a brief pause he asked, "What happened?"

They all pitched in to tell the story. Pop shook his head. Hearing the description of the ghost blocking the way, he knew it had to have been old Hezekia Pittee.

Jack was icing down his bruised wrists and arms while Kai was busy tending to his very sore feet and shoulders. It finally occurred to Jack that Kai had protected him from a disastrous end and had risked his own life in the process.

"How long were you hanging on to my ankle?"

"I don't know? Seemed like forever. Don't make a big deal out of it. The good news is, I think maybe I got a couple inches taller," said Kai.

"Yeah, well, I owe you big time, which kinda sucks," laughed Jack.

"So now we jus' split the gold sixty forty. How's that?"

Val's ears perked up. "What are you talking about? What gold?"

"Maybe it's time to call it a night," interrupted Pop as he stood suddenly. He knew Kai had just blown their big secret and was trying valiantly to give the boys a way to escape the barrage of questions sure to be headed their way.

"Wait a minute," Nan jumped in. "Is there something going on that we should know about?"

Pop cleared his throat and started backing away toward the safety of his beloved study, wondering how many days he could survive locked away without coffee and cigars. He finally decided to put on the tough guy act and take his chances. "Well, that's a two part question and can be answered with a yes *and* a no. Yes, you could probably say somethin's goin' on and no, no one needs to know about it. Least not yet. I guess. Maybe." Pop was trying to figure out a way to disappear like one of the ghosts. His tough guy approach was about as doomed as he was.

"Oh no you don't. You're not getting away with that line. Have you got these two on some wild goose chase treasure hunt?" asked Nan.

Kai bumbled on. "It's not a wild goose chase. Pop doesn't know it yet, but we found the box filled with the gold this afternoon."

The secret was out and all eyes immediately turned toward Jack, as he slumped forward with a groan preparing to explain.

11

Blabbermouth

"You're telling me that these boys have been out digging around in the marsh on Rattle Snake Island searching for some stupid treasure chest?" asked Nan.

"Well, honey, yeah, I guess, but they're fine. It's not really a treasure chest anyway, it's just an old box, filled with gold pieces an' maybe some gemstones," answered Pop lamely.

"Don't you think *maybe* a place called Rattlesnake Island might be just a little bit dangerous? Did you happen to think of *that* while you were coaching them along? How about the fact that they're digging in some ancient Indian burial ground? Nothing crossed your mind there either?" Nan wasn't very happy.

"Whoa… wait a minute. You just went nose to nose with some creepy dead guy. Since when did you become some shrinkin' violet?" replied Pop defiantly.

"Since I almost lost my grandson"

Pop couldn't come up with a comeback for that one.

"Don't worry about it. I'll make sure everything's covered so no one gets hurt. I wouldn't let them get into somethin' I thought was too risky," answered Pop.

Nan wasn't convinced but agreed to let it drop for the time being. In the great room, the debate was going on in much the same way. Val and Talia, after their own scary ordeal, were not enthused. They were particularly upset when told that the next stage of the task would have to be carried out at night. When the boys explained that Pop was not going to be with them, the girls protested even louder, insisting that the danger was too great.

"Nice one Kai" said Jack as he rolled his eyes. "We're back to a fifty-fifty split."

"Hey, man, I'm sorry. I wasn't thinkin'. I really blew it this time," replied Kai.

"We have to finalize our plan and get this over with before Nan talks about it with my Mom. She would freak out for sure."

Talia interrupted them. "Your mom should freak out. It's a crazy idea no matter how much gold is in that box."

"Well, now that I'm calmed down and since you guys are so stubborn, I was thinking that maybe we could help somehow," offered Val.

Everyone turned, looking at Val, waiting for her to explain further.

"Really, think about it. It's obvious there's more to it than just the two of you can handle. If we all pitched in…... "

"Okay, so what, exactly could you guys do to help us out there?" asked Kai sincerely.

"I'm not sure, but you said you had to dig at night, so someone will have to hold lights and someone will need to stay with the boat in case there's any trouble. Besides, the box might be heavy….."

"That's what we're hoping for, a heavy box," interrupted Jack.

"You guys are making this sound way too simple," Talia complained.

Jack was irritated with the way the conversation was going. "Wait a minute. We're capable of handling this ourselves. I appreciate the offer Val, but it's not like we're scared about going into the marsh at night. There are no ghosts out *there,* or anything else for that matter. That would be just what we would need in the middle of the night, an expedition crew, like something from National Geographic. We might as well have news cameras zooming in on us for crying out loud. This has to be done low key and we're going to get this done our way."

Talia wouldn't let it drop. "You didn't think anything would happen at the lighthouse either…"

"Cheap shot!" howled Kai with a smirk. "What the heck, we got through tonight with just a few scrapes an' there wasn't even any treasure to collect. We'll be fine, stop worryin' like a couple of old la….. uh…. girls."

They finally reached their first agreement since leaving the lighthouse when they decided it was time to crash for the night. Daylight was fast approaching and everyone's nerves were frayed. The debate could continue in the morning. Val and Talia, still chattering away, went off to one of the guest rooms as the boys dragged their way to the boathouse.

The next morning, while the girls were still asleep, Jack walked into Pop's study with
a cup of coffee in each hand. He wanted to talk about what they had found as well as his plan for retrieving the Cresson fortune, hopefully, without further interference. Pop was still upset about his good friend being banged up, but relieved to know that Mr. Farrell was going to be fine after a couple of days rest. Jack could tell that Pop was distracted so he waited patiently for the conversation to wind around slowly to the topic of the buried box.

"So what are you doin' up so early Jackman?" questioned Pop as Jack eased into one of the plush leather chairs.

"I knew you were in here and thought maybe you'd want some company and another cup of coffee. Everyone else is still zonked out."

"I could always do with some company, 'specially if it's you pal," answered Pop.

"Well, I'm sorry about your friend. I feel like it's my fault in a way."

"Nonsense. You don't need to feel guilty. John n' me go back a long ways and he'd be the first to say that none of it had anything to do with you kids. He just wasn't prepared for what he saw when he went inside. You'd think after him tellin' all of those stories for years n' years, he wouldn't have been so shocked. Of course, I didn't see what he did, so I guess I can't really make a fair judgment."

"How did Nan handle that ghost like she did Pop?"

"That's easy. The only thing she had on her mind was gettin' to you. Nothin', not even the ghost of Hezekia Pittee was gonna stop her." Pop chuckled. "Heck, even I know when to get outta her way. I'll bet the poor bugger got the same look I got when I bought that wooden boat. It probably scared the ....well, you know what I mean."

"I guess we have a problem now since Kai blabbed about our little project. We're never gonna get a chance to go after it with everyone being so freaked out."

"You'll get your chance. Just don't mention it to anyone for a bit and let things settle down."

"The thing is, we know exactly where it is, and the dirt is already loose at the box. We could be over there and back with the gold in a couple of hours," said Jack.

"That's all well n' good. I want you to be confident, not cocky. Now you're being cocky. Things can *always* go wrong. You have to have a plan B," said Pop.

"So you think we should just wait until the whole lighthouse nightmare blows over?"

"That's what I'd do. At least wait 'til you're not so sore, but don't wait too long, I might run over there and grab it myself," Pop teased.

"Maybe we'll go snatch it in a couple of days. I checked the tide chart yesterday and it will be high tide around ten o'clock on Wednesday night. That would be perfect. I'll be able to get *Bad Latitude* pretty close to shore without hitting the bottom. At high tide we'll have almost four feet of water." Jack was excited again.

"Sounds reasonable to me. Did you happen to notice what kind of shape the box was in? I would think that after three hundred years, it would be pretty well rotted."

Jack thought about it for a minute. "You know, I didn't really check it out. I don't have any idea what kind of shape it's in. We only scraped off the dirt on top of it. Since we had the kayaks, we couldn't carry it back anyway so we just covered it back up."

"May I humbly suggest you take a few heavy canvas bags so you can load the loot from the box to the bags? It'll make it easier to handle if it turns out to be heavy and you have to divide it up. It won't matter then if the box is rotted. Besides, a canvas sack won't beat up your boat," said Pop.

"Great idea. Do you think it would be better if you went with us?"

"Do you want me to go?"

"I think it would be great…."

"But you would prefer doing it yourself," interrupted Pop.

Jack smiled. No way was he getting anything past Pop. "Yeah, I guess I'd rather be able to say that I sorta did this on my own."

Pop laughed out loud. "Good. I would have been disappointed if you had answered any other way. Now, do us all a favor and keep this quiet. Don't even tell Kai when you're gonna dig 'til the night you do it. That way, he can't start the ball rollin' again. Got it?"

"Got it," grinned Jack as he left the study.

Kai was still passed out but the girls were wide awake, sitting on the porch drinking coffee with Nan. Even with her hair messed up and wearing a borrowed robe, Jack couldn't help but notice how great Talia looked. She smiled shyly as she seemed to read his mind.

"Good morning ladies," greeted Jack as he entered the porch. "You're all looking especially fine in your designer jammies," he chuckled.

"Watch out girls. He's been busy conniving with the old geezer. Don't let him charm you into thinking nothing's going on. I know those two too well. He's just like his dad this one," said Nan with one eyebrow raised, trying unsuccessfully to suppress a smile.

"Awwww, c'mon Nan. That's not fair. You're gonna give them the wrong impression about me," whined Jack playfully.

"Yeah right. After last night, I don't think I need to warn these girls about your daredevil maneuvers. You've got something up your sleeve. I can feel it," answered Nan.

Kai walked out to join everyone. He shuffled with a noticeable limp and both feet were bruised below the ankles. His eyes were puffy and his curls pointed wildly in all directions. Val giggled as he collapsed onto the wicker settee.

"The truck that ran over you, must have backed up to do it again," announced Nan. "I think you need some breakfast."

"What I need is a spa and a massage. Geez, every muscle in my body hurts."

"At least you won't be able to go grave digging for awhile," added Talia. She was sorry she said it as soon as the words were out.

Jack shook his head but resisted the urge to reply. He was going to try to keep the conversation about the treasure off the table for as long as possible. If they all thought they couldn't do any digging now, all the better.

Val jumped up and moved next to Kai. She examined his bruises and started rubbing his shoulders to loosen the tight muscles. He tensed as Val hit the sorest spots but she continued and, after a few minutes, she felt him relax.

"Why don't we all just go to the beach and lay out in the sun for the day," Val suggested. "I think the sun and salt water would help you guys feel better. It will be a good way to chill."

"I think that's a great idea but, with my luck, I'll fall asleep and burn like a strip of bacon," complained Kai.

"Well Porky, I think we should do whatever Dr. Val orders. It would do all of us some good," answered Jack. "What do you think Talia? Beach day?"

"I think it's the best idea I've heard in days," she replied.

While the kids were hanging out at the beach, Pop was busy walking across Rattlesnake Island surveying the area in search of problems. He used the deck boat to get as close to the island as possible and waded through the last fifteen feet between the boat and shore. After an hour stomping through the high grass, he decided there were plenty of reasons for worry, most of them slithering ones. There were more snakes than he remembered from his visit ten years earlier. It was bad enough during daylight hours, but it would be impossible to see them once it turned dark. Maybe, he thought, the boys should take their chances during the day and hope for the best. While that idea was running through his mind, he noticed a small boat circling offshore. Whoever was in the boat was very curious about what he was up to. He walked back toward the deck boat and waved to the boater as he reached the shoreline, convinced beyond any doubt that the dig would have to be done at night, as originally planned.

"What the heck are you doing out there?" asked the nosy boater.

Pop knew he had to say something to satisfy the guy's curiosity while scaring him off the trail. "My wife is a nature photographer and I heard there were lots of snakes out here. I just decided to check it out for myself."

"Really? Did you find any?"

"Man, the place is crawlin' with 'em. Rattlers, Pygmies, Moccasins, you name it. She's gonna have a field day," Pop yelled out, pretending to be excited.

"You've got to be kidding. They're all poisonous!" replied the boater.

Duh! This guys a real genius.

"Yeah, I know. She likes to get close ups of their colors and then stirs 'em up to get shots of 'em tryin' to strike. You should see her pictures, they're fantastic."

The boater threw up his hands and moved behind the helm. "Good luck buddy. Sounds like you're married to a real nut."

The roar of the outboard drowned out Pop's laugh as he waded to the boat. To no one but himself he muttered, "Yeah Pal, I'd pay big bucks to see you say that to her face."

12

Burial Grounds

Following a few of days of surfing, tourist rides on the St. Augustine trolley and several rounds of miniature golf, it was time to begin the final leg of the big quest. Jack was determined to recover the fortune before everyone grew suspicious again. He wanted to take advantage of the timing of the high tide and went over the details of his plan with Pop one last time. As Pop suggested, he didn't tell Kai they were going to the island until an hour before dusk. Nan was busy visiting with friends. She wouldn't notice *Bad Latitude* missing from the lift. The weather was perfect with just the hint of a breeze. With a little luck, they would be downriver and back before anyone knew they had ever left.

Jack had packed everything they might need and loaded his boat with the canvas bags, rope, shovels, and two powerful spotlights. The deck was covered with rubber mats to protect it from damage. A large ice chest was loaded onboard and would be used to float the tools across the shallow water as they waded to shore. Pop had insisted they wear long sleeves and leather gloves to go with the rubber boots. He was extremely worried about the snakes.

Traveling at half throttle with the running lights on, Jack was being very deliberate with the timing of their arrival. He wanted to be in the vicinity just before dark, but preferred to anchor once darkness fell. As they approached Rattlesnake Island, he was relieved to find there were no other boats in sight. He snapped on the overhead light mounted on the back rail of the T-top and positioned the stern facing the shoreline. Carefully watching the depth finder, he was able to get the boat to within fifteen feet of the riverbank. They were in three feet of water and the tide was coming in. There would be at least four feet of water to wade through once they returned. Jack let the motor idle while Kai secured the bow anchor. Once it gripped the bottom, another anchor was put off the stern, to keep the boat positioned for a quick exit. The boys went about their work quietly, as if it had all been rehearsed.

Jack mounted the ladder onto the gunwale and climbed over the side into the water. When he had his footing, he nodded and Kai handed him the cooler filled with equipment. The running lights were left on to comply with boating regulations, but Kai extinguished the stern light to avoid attracting the attention of passing boaters. After checking the anchors one last time, Kai joined Jack in the water and they waded toward shore together.

Using the cooler as a toolbox worked perfectly. On shore, Kai began shining the spotlight in a sweeping motion across the ground, keeping an eye out for snakes. While he played lookout, Jack put on his boots and gloves, then took over the lookout duties while Kai geared up. The shovels, rope, canvas bags, and spotlights were removed from the cooler and Jack turned on the GPS for their trek through the waste deep marsh grasses. The moon was bright and visibility was good, maybe too good. Both guys tried to push the nagging worries of the burial grounds from their minds, while animal noises and the sound of their own breathing was amplified over the stillness.

It took ten minutes to find the dig location. The GPS gadget guided them to within two feet of their marker. Removal of the transplanted grass, used to hide the spot, was the first order of business.

"You aim the lights and watch our backs and I'll do the digging," instructed Jack.

"Why don't we split the diggin' up?"

Jack went to work with the folding shovel. "I'll be okay. Your shoulders and feet are still killing you. The dirt's still loose so it should be easy. Pop wants one of us to watch out for snakes at all times. We can't watch and dig at the same time so you'll have to keep an eye out. You've also gotta make sure nobody goes nosing around the boat. Your job is as important as the digging and your head's gonna have to be on a swivel."

"Hey, that's okay with me. I just wanna do my part. I ain't along for the ride, you know."

"I'm telling you, you're not along for the ride. I'm depending on you to help keep things safe. You can do some of the grunt work when we carry the gold to the boat."

Kai didn't press the issue. He was still sore and understood the need for caution. "I'm not so afraid of snakes but you know what really grosses me out?" he asked.

"I don't know, Willie n' Billy, maybe?"

"Yeah, them too, but I was talkin' about animals."

"They seem like animals to me," quipped Jack.

"Okay, okay, you're right, they are, but I mean the four legged kind of animals."

"Hey, they were on all fours in the middle of town."

Kai sighed. "You always gotta have some kind of answer. Can I please make my point?"

"Sorry. Go ahead. Tell me what animal grosses you out more than....Stop! Don't move! Don't even breathe! You weren't paying attention for snakes and now there's one coiled up behind your left foot. He ain't a pygmy either." Jack was whispering while pointing.

Kai's eyes bulged in terror as he froze in place. Very slowly, he turned his head toward his left boot.

"Stop! I'm telling you. You can't move. Can't you hear that rattle? Let me get the shovel and see if I can scare him off." Jack appeared panicked.

"Jack, what if I just take one big jump to the right. Don't go swingin' that shovel at it. If you miss, I'm bit."

"Listen up. Dive headfirst to your right and roll as soon as you land. First let me shine this light around to make sure there's no little snake brothers or sisters waiting for you."

"Okay, hurry up, I'm gettin' a cramp." Kai's voice was cracking now.

"It's all clear. On three. One. Two Three!"

Kai followed the instructions to the letter and Jack dropped to his knees in hysterics.

Gasping and shaking, Kai looked disgustedly toward Jack as he picked himself up. He bent forward placing both hands on his knees gasping for breath.

"Whaddya laughin' at you moron? I was inches from death."

Jack had tears streaming down his cheeks and his stomach muscles ached. "You're calling me a moron? It wasn't me rolling around down there. I can't believe you fell for that."

Kai stared in disbelief. "You mean *that* was a joke? I almost peed my pants you idiot."

"I'm sorry. I shouldn't joke out here, but you set it up and I had to do it," Jack laughed.

Kai couldn't help but snicker. "Rackham, you're freakin' unbelievable. A real comedian. I can't believe you dogged me like that. Hope you don't think I'm not gonna get even."

"I'm sure you will. Really though, we shouldn't mess around out here. There are a gazillion snakes and we need to pay attention," said Jack in a deliberately serious tone.

"Armadillos."

"What about armadillos?"

"Armadillos gross me out. They're just big rats with armor on 'em," complained Kai.

"You're absolutely amazing. I have no idea how your brain can change gears like it does," Jack chuckled. "Hey, whaddya think. Should we get busy so we can get back? No more practical jokes though until we get outta here. Okay?"

"Yeah, no more jokin' around. Besides, this place is startin' to creep me out."

Jack was busy again digging. It didn't take long until he was knee deep in the long forgotten grave. Kai aimed one light into the pit while scanning the area with the other light. Every now and then, he would sneak a peek around his own feet. Jack smiled to himself every time his friend did the not so discreet foot check.

After climbing out of the hole Jack banked back the edges to make sure the soils wouldn't collapse. He tossed a length of rope into the gravesite to use as a lifeline, just in case the worst happened, and jumped into the pit one more time. An hour after starting, most of the skeleton was visible on the back side of the grave. Nearing the bottom, he tried to dig away from the Indian King, but the soils were sandy and crumbled away from the yellowed bones. Kai was getting jumpier as more of the skeleton was exposed.

"Can't you throw some dirt over those bones? I'm not likin' havin' to look at that dead guy sharin' space with you in there," Kai griped as he flashed the light between Jack and the buried King.

"Hey, it won't be long now and he's not going anywhere. He's dead. Remember? I can't help it if the dirt's falling in off of him."

"Yeah, well hurry up. It's like he's watchin' us n' just waitin' to pounce on you."

"C'mon, stop whining. Another five minutes at most. Just keep your eyes peeled for boaters and snakes and I'll be outta here with the loot."

Finally, Jack scraped the top of the box and hurriedly dug around the rectangular outline.

"Got it! Shine that other light down here and let's see what we've got," yelled Jack.

Kai knelt down at the edge and peered below with the spot light. As Pop had suggested, the box was in bad shape and would be impossible to carry.

"Do me a favor, throw me that pry bar down here. Might as well see what we've got."

Kai grabbed the bar and handed it down while aiming the second light onto the box. He had forgotten to scan the area for snakes or any other visitors. Both were now completely absorbed in their work, trying to uncover the contents of the box. Jack jammed the bar into the top edges of the chest. After a couple of tries, the rotted wood gave way and the top ripped away from the frame.

"I think we hit pay dirt pal. Chuck one of those lights down here."

As they hoped, the box was crammed with gold coins, chains and hundreds of precious gemstones. They had finally done it. Kai did a quick scan for snakes, took a sneak peek toward the boat, and hurriedly tossed the canvas bags into the grave. Jack filled them with the treasure as Kai watched excitedly from above.

"Whaddya think its all worth?" asked Kai.

"I have no idea. All I know is it's gotta be worth millions. This is incredible! Check out all these emeralds and rubies. They're huge! I can't believe that Cresson guy could've carried all this stuff as far as he did. It had to be a seventy-five mile hike.

Jack divided the heavy contents into three bags. He carefully tied the top of each bag with a short piece of rope. With the tops secured, he tied them all together and looped them through the larger safety rope already coiled at the bottom of the hole. It would be easier if he and Kai pulled the bags up together. There was no way to carry all three of them at the same time while trying to climb from the collapsing pit. Once the bags were ready to go, Jack dug a few shallow handholds to make his exit to the top easier. That done, he tossed the shovel and the spotlight out of the hole and started pulling himself up the side as Kai lit the way.

Jack was on his belly with his waist bent at the edge of the pit, when Kai freaked out.

"Get outta there! Get outta there! It came to life! It's tryin' to get you!" Kai screamed.

"Yeah right," Jack laughed. "Thought we said no jokes 'til we got off the island." He had just started pushing himself up to his knees.

"Hurry up! I'm not kiddin'! I swear! Hurry! Hurry!" Kai was jumping up and down as Jack reluctantly turned expecting another prank.

Kai was running to the opposite side of the hole trying to reach Jack. The light flashed wildly as he ran. The combination of the moonlight and the moving spotlight cast a creepy background for the sight that Jack confronted. At that very moment, the wind began to howl and the sound of loud movement could be heard approaching their position from beyond the line of palmettos to their east.

Pain exploded in the back of Jack's leg, just below the knee, as he tried to scramble the last few feet to escape the ancient grave. The long dead warrior had grabbed Jack's calf in a vice-like grip with its skeletal hand, tugging hard, trying to stand. The pain was incredible and Jack dug his fingers into the soft soils clawing desperately to keep from falling backwards to join the partially buried corpse, while the noise from the line of palmettos grew steadily louder and the smell of rotten meat filled the air.

13

Val's Intuition

It was nine thirty. Val wasn't sure how, but she knew Kai and Jack were on the island and that they were in serious danger. What she didn't know was what to do about it. If she called and shared her worries with Nan, she knew the guys would be furious with her. Confiding in Talia would be no help at all. Still, something was wrong and she couldn't sit by and do nothing. Finally, she called the Rackham's and was relieved when it was Pop that answered the phone. If anyone knew their whereabouts, he would.

"Hi, it's Val. Is Jack there?" she asked.

"Hello there Valerie. No, he's not home right now."

"Uh, I didn't think he would be. I'm, uh, kinda worried about something."

"What are you worried about kid?" Pop could hear genuine concern in her voice.

"Well, I think Jack and Kai are on that island and I have a really bad feeling that something's wrong. I just don't know what to do," Val's voice was quivering slightly.

"Val, everything's fine. You're gettin' all worked up over nothin'."

"No, something's definitely wrong, I know it. I never get like this. If they were on the island, would you tell me?"

"Yeah, they're over there," Pop replied.

"Do you know where they are exactly? Could we go see if everything's okay?"

Pop decided that a quick trip to check things out might be a good idea. Val was a good kid, not one to get upset easily. This was one time when following a hunch made sense. His hunch said that maybe Val's intuition was in overdrive but deserved attention.

"Val, how long will it take you to get here?"

"Five minutes."

"Okay, come on over. I'm gonna get the boat ready and you n' me will take a ride over there." Pop was trying to mask any sound of worry in his voice.

"See you in a few minutes. Uh, I know maybe I'm sounding silly but really, I appreciate you listening to me."

"No problem. Now hurry along. I'm goin' down to the boat dock now." Pop broke the connection and hustled out to the boathouse.

Val arrived five minutes later and hurried through the back yard to the dock. Pop had the Hurricane idling in the water, ready to go. She hopped aboard and they were off in seconds. Still feeling slightly embarrassed, she thanked Pop again for taking her seriously.

"There's nothin' crazy or silly about intuition Val. You didn't know they were goin' over there tonight, so there must be somethin' to it. If you have a bad feelin' about this, then we need to check it out. If everything's okay, we'll just end up takin' a little nighttime boat cruise," said Pop.

The truth was, Pop was concerned and was trying to mix caution with speed to get to the island in a hurry. Fifteen minutes had passed since Val first called and they were still five minutes away. The ride seemed to take forever but finally, *Bad Latitude* came into view.

Pop nosed the deck boat in as tight to shore as he dared and tossed the anchor onto the riverbank. He was wearing jeans, a pair of Justin boots and a sleeveless T-shirt. He wished he had heeded his own advice and brought gloves and a long sleeved shirt.

"Val, now listen carefully. Keep these spot lights aimed straight ahead like this," he demonstrated. "This, over here on the helm, is the button for the boat horn. If anything even looks weird, don't be bashful about it, just sound it a couple of times and I'll be right back. Oh, and by the way, don't leave this boat no matter what you see or hear. You got that?"

Without waiting for a reply, Pop was over the side, plowing toward shore. He stopped long enough to secure the anchor in the muddy bank and, flashlight in hand, walked briskly in the direction where he knew Jack and Kai would be digging. Snakes were no longer a concern as his priority was getting from point A to point B as quickly as possible. Something had to be up. The sound of Pop's boat motor and the shining flashlight from the shoreline should have caused the boys to investigate by at least shining their lights toward Jack's boat.

It took less than sixty seconds for Pop to see a light flashing about wildly. He began to sprint. To his left, he caught the distinct sound of movement from the line of brush and palmettos. Ignoring the noise, he continued toward the wild light. As he approached, he could see Jack struggling to climb out of the gravesite while Kai reached over the side swinging a spotlight at something inside the pit. Finally, Pop saw the skeletal hand of the buried Indian clamped onto his grandson's leg.

There was no time to waste. Pop grabbed one of the folding shovels and leaped to the opposite side of the grave. He raised the shovel over his head as he jumped. His aim was perfect and the shovel's edge arced toward the bony wrist. As the shovel sliced its way downward, Kai caught a glimpse of the chopping motion and let out a panicked yell.

The brittle bone was no match for the brute force behind the swing and the shovel knifed through the wrist above the joint with ease. With a tremendous backhanded swing, Pop cracked the shovel across the skull of the buried King, causing the head to break loose from the spine. The skeleton buckled in half at the waist to lie motionless within the grave.

Jack rolled from the edge of the pit, just as the side of the hole collapsed, partially filling the excavation, while completely covering the bags filled with the treasure. Only the end of the rope was visible.

Kai crawled over and fell onto his back next to Jack. He stared up at Pop and grinned. "All I saw was that shovel headin' down at my head like an axe an' all I could think of was *"Now What!"* panted Kai.

"Yeah, well we can talk about it later. Let's get movin'. There's somethin' out here and it's walkin' or crawlin' this way. Val's waitin' in the boat," answered Pop catching his breath.

Jack finally spoke up. "What's Val doing here?"

"She figured out that you guys were over here and had a bad feeling about things. I decided to trust her instincts and we buzzed over to check up on the two of you. Looks like it turned out to be the right call. You can thank her for savin' your butts when we get back."

"Look, the rope is sticking out. I could dig enough loose so that the three of us could pull the bags out," said Jack. "There's somethin' in those palmettos and we're not hangin' around. Hurry up. Let's throw some dirt and grass over this hole, and get outta here. We'll figure out what to do about the gold later. C'mon, hustle up." Pop wasn't in the mood to debate and began shoveling dirt into the crater.

Jack attempted to stand, but clutched at his leg and fell in a heap to the ground. The bony hand was still clamped onto his calf. Pop moved quickly, and knelt at Jack's side to see what was wrong. Shaking his head, he grasped the claw-like hand between his own mitt-like hands and pried it open with little apparent effort. Jack let out a pained sigh as the gouging pressure was released and Pop tossed the severed hand into the grave and resumed shoveling.

"We'll have to check you out at home. I don't see any blood, but you're gonna have a really bad bruise there. Gather up your gear while we finish up. This hole will be hidden in a few minutes and then we're on our way," said Pop as he looked again toward the palmetto line. The sounds had died down, but the movement continued slowly in their direction. Pop figured time was running out and wasn't in the mood to confront some new threat.

Jack helped spread the grasses over the dirt and made sure the rope was hidden. He was frustrated to have gotten so close only to leave empty-handed. The movement to the east sounded closer and he grabbed a light to shine in the direction of the noise. Pop grabbed his arm as he started to turn the light toward the palmettos.

"Let's leave well enough alone. Whatever it is, I don't want to aggravate it. We're gonna get out of here and get the next move figured out when we get home." Pop used a tone that left no room for discussion.

Jack turned abruptly, grabbed one of the shovels, and stalked off without waiting for Pop or Kai, muttering something under his breath as he stomped away. They walked quickly through the grass with no further conversation. When they were within several yards of shore, Pop motioned to Kai to go on ahead just before ordering Jack to stop. Jack knew he was in trouble when Pop grabbed the collar of his shirt and yanked him practically off his feet until they were facing one another chest-to-chest.

Pop was angry and wagged a finger inches from Jack's face. "Jackson, you cop an attitude with me like that again, and you'll be on a northbound plane, and you'll never be allowed to stay at our place again. You got that?"

"Yeah, I'm sorry Pop."

"You'd better be. I've told you before; disrespect is somethin' I won't tolerate, not from you or anybody else. Get as disgusted as you want, just cut the crap, and keep your lousy attitude to yourself."

Pop let go of the shirt, brushed his way past, and walked to the Hurricane's anchor. This was uncharted territory for Jack. It wasn't the first time he had gotten in trouble, but he couldn't remember a time when his grandfather had been so totally enraged. He dragged his feet while wading to the boat, hoping for the slightest trace of mellowing. Pop ignored him as he climbed aboard the Hurricane and started the engine. Jack was still climbing the boat ladder when Pop and Val pulled away.

Kai retrieved the bow anchor while Jack fired up the boat. Once the anchor was on board, Jack backed the boat toward shore to take the slack out of the stern line. Wordlessly he reeled in the stern anchor and carefully stowed it on the rubber mat. *Bad Latitude* moved slowly toward the center of the river as Kai joined him at the helm.

"Nice move butt head. The man shows up outta nowhere to save our rear ends and you gotta act like some punk."

"Just shut up Kai. I know I screwed up but I don't need to listen to you run your mouth."

"Okay. I'll shut up. I forgot. Nobody can ever say anything to you."

"Listen will you? It's not like that. I'm just…"

"Bull. Now I don't wanna hear it. I just wanna get back to the dock so me n' Val can leave. As usual, you know it all," answered Kai as he moved forward to the bow.

Jack tried again to apologize and square things up with his friend, but Kai had made up his mind. After a few attempts, he gave up and they rode to the dock in awkward silence. The night had gone from bad to worse. Jack knew it wasn't finished. There was nothing worse than one of Pop's lectures, but seeing the rare display of temper had to be a close second.

They arrived at the dock to find Pop and Val hosing off the deck boat. Kai offloaded the gear, carelessly stacking everything in a heap. He was in a rush to make himself scarce at the earliest possible moment. Val looked anxious to leave as well. The clean up was done in ten minutes and Val and Kai were quietly on their way. Jack felt abandoned but knew he had no one to blame but himself. After getting cleaned up and changed, he limped into the house to apologize and make things right. After a ten-minute search, he found Pop sitting on the deck above the boathouse smoking one of his nasty cigars.

"Pop, I'm really sorry I acted like a jerk, but I was just so frustrated…"

"Using the word *but* in an apology is just a way to imply that you had an excuse for acting the way you did. I don't buy it. You had no idea what you might have been up against out there. Nan and I give you more freedom than probably makes sense sometimes, but only 'cause we feel like you're mature enough, and smart enough, to be trusted," said Pop.

He's practically breathing fire.

"By now you're figurin' you're in for a major lecture. You're figurin' wrong. I'll just tell you this one time. Respect is a foundation for everything in life. You'll get nowhere being disrespectful to others and that includes family, teachers, and even your friends."

Pop stood up, gazed out over the waterway, and cleared his throat. He was struggling with another thought and trying to decide exactly what to say and how. Jack used the pause to try apologizing again, this time minus the use of the word *but*.

"Pop, I don't have any excuse. I shouldn't have acted that way with you. You were there looking out for us and I blew it. There's nothing else to say other than I'm sorry and I'll never let it happen again."

"Your apology is accepted. I know you're a great kid and you usually show pretty good judgment, but I'm concerned about this treasure hunt business and the way you've been actin'. You're completely obsessed with it, to the point that you'd be willin' to stay out there, with whatever's on that island, and take some stupid risk." Pop walked to the steps, stopped at the landing, and turned to face his grandson. He looked sad and tired.

"I don't want you and Kai on that island again. I think it's best that the gold be left alone. It's not worth your lives."

Without further pause, Pop trudged down the wooden stairs, leaving Jack alone with his thoughts and a very sore leg.

14

The Pirate's Den

Talia wandered alone through the ancient city. It was a warm morning under a bright azure sky. Only her mood was dark as she thought about the way her summer was ending. For a time, it seemed that she and Jack could be a couple, but his obsession with the treasure hunt had turned her hopes into disappointment. Time was running out. She would be leaving soon to join her family, and might never see him again.

After stopping at *The Java Hut*, where she ordered a large sugar free vanilla latte, Talia crossed the street, and sat down on an empty stone bench on the walkway overlooking the St. Augustine harbor. The spot provided a pleasant view of the old fort, the inlet, and the *Bridge of Lions*. There was the slight hint of an ocean breeze, and several boats were cruising slowly through the waterway. The setting and the weather would have been perfect, if not for her sense of loneliness.

To her left she noticed a pod of dolphins circling, several yards from the seawall. After a short time, they began swimming toward the northern end of the harbor, in the direction of the inlet. Following their progress with her gaze, she spotted a familiar looking boat anchored near the coquina bulkhead in front of the fort. The bow was facing north and the name was hidden, but she was sure that it was Jack's. Tossing the empty coffee cup into the trash can, she walked along the seawall toward the Castillo, trying not to get her hopes up.

It was *Bad Latitude*, but no one was aboard. The boat sparkled in the morning sun against the reflecting background of the sea green water. Talia scanned the area hoping to spot Jack nearby. She had spoken with Val the day before and knew that he and Kai were at odds with one another and she worried that Jack wanted to be left alone. After several minutes of searching with no success, she sat on the wall facing the boat, waiting for his return. She didn't have to wait long.

From behind came a familiar voice. "Is anyone sitting here?"

Talia turned and smiled but stumbled trying to stand. Jack helped her to her feet, practically picking her up, with no sign of effort. Slightly embarrassed by her clumsiness, she started to say hello, but never got the chance. Before both feet were firmly planted on the ground, she felt his arms wrapped around her shoulders and his lips pressed firmly against her own. Closing her eyes, hoping it wasn't a silly daydream, she returned his kiss.

"Wow, what was that all about?" she asked breathlessly.

"That was something I should have done weeks ago. When I saw you sitting here, in the same place where I first saw you, I decided this was it."

"So why did it take you so long?" she laughed.

"I guess I was nervous, maybe even stupid."

"I can understand nervous but why stupid?"

Jack paused before answering. "I got so caught up with getting that gold off the island, I ended up treating everyone I care about like they really didn't matter, including you. Even Pop is mad at me now, and that never happens."

"I heard. Val told me."

"Yeah, if it weren't for Val, me n' Kai would be toast. She and Pop showed up just in time. Instead of listening to Pop, I acted like a creep. Now he doesn't want me going near the place."

"Well, I'm sure he'll calm down about it in a few days."

"I don't think so. I've never seen him so ticked off."

"Just let it go. You'll see. It'll all work out." Talia was trying to sound reassuring. After her conversation with Val, she had her doubts and part of her hoped Pop would stick to his decision. She never liked the idea of the guys being on the island at night, even less now that something had tried to grab Jack. What she really wanted was the chance to spend some time with him alone before leaving for her new home.

"So, you want to go for a spin on the boat?" asked Jack.

"Sure, but you're anchored out there in the water. How do I get onboard without getting totally soaked?"

"That's no problem. It's only three or four feet deep. You hop up on my shoulders and I'll carry you. When we get there, I'll turn backwards and you slide your butt onto the gunwale. Simple".

Talia giggled. "Yeah, sounds simple. We're gonna look simple."

"Who cares? It's either that or you can swim or I can pick you up at the dock half a mile down the road. Your choice."

116

"I guess I'll go for looking simple, but let's get going before anyone sees us."

They climbed from the wall to the water's edge. Jack pulled off his shirt, wrapped his wallet inside, and handed the bundle to Talia before crouching to let her climb onto his shoulder. Taking care to keep his footing, Jack waded out to *Bad Latitude*. As they approached the boat, early visitors of the Castillo were yelling out words of encouragement, mixed with a few whistles and off color comments. As promised, the water was only chest-deep and transferring her from his shoulders onto the gunwale proved easy.

"Now let's see how easy it is for you to get in," teased Talia.

"No problem," replied Jack with a smirk. He planted both hands on the gunwale, flexed his legs, and rocketed out of the water. He was onboard in a blink, his feet never touching the side. Talia noticed his bulging biceps and forearms and smiled.

"So where to?" asked Jack as he started the engine.

"I don't know. You're the Captain remember?"

Jack collected the anchor and stowed it inside the locker. He moved to the helm and piloted the boat through the moored cruisers and sailboats. Within a few minutes, they were running at full speed toward the ocean. *Bad Latitude* cut through the inlet past the jetties and into the Atlantic. A quarter mile offshore, he took a northerly heading and cut the throttle back to two thirds. The seas were relatively calm, running at two to three feet, just enough chop to cause an uncomfortable bounce operating at full speed.

"So Cap'n, where are we going?"

"I was thinking Fernandina Beach, up at Amelia Island."

"Is it a long ride?"

"Yeah, it's probably a good thirty five miles up the coast."

"Cool. I was hoping it would be."

"That means you're stuck with me, all alone, for the rest of the day."

"Do we have enough gas to go that far and back?" asked Talia.

"I topped off the tank this morning. This boat carries one hundred and twenty gallons of fuel. If the seas stay like this, we can make it up and back and have ninety gallons to spare."

The offshore ride took a little under two hours. They reached the inlet at Cumberland Sound just after eleven-thirty.

"Over there to the right is Georgia. That's Cumberland Island and just north of that is Jekyll Island. This whole area was once a pirate hangout, especially Fernandina, the town where we're going to be visiting," explained Jack as he steered into the mouth of the Amelia River.

"They also call this the Isle of Eight Flags because during its nearly five hundred year history, it was governed by eight different nations. Naturally, they all flew their own flags while the area was under their control. The pirate Luis Aury once claimed it for Mexico in the early 1800's."

"Somehow I can picture you as a pirate," said Talia. "You have that mix of intensity, curiosity, and fearlessness that they all must have had."

"Arrhhhgg lassie, ye may be right. Don't forget, I have to make my ancestors proud. My intensity and sense of adventure drives my poor mom absolutely nuts. She would freak if she knew that you and me just traveled this far up the coast in this boat all by ourselves."

"That's funny. Your mom seemed really easy going about things."

"Normally she is. I think she decided a long time ago that this family was a bunch of crazies and had no choice but to roll along with it all. She and Pop have had a few chats about what he lets me do down here. He always exaggerates his stories about what I'm up to and just about gives her panic attacks. Nan always smoothes things over and then gives Pop an earful about teasing my mom like that."

"Your dad doesn't get upset?"

"Whaddya kidding? I only spend summers here with them. My dad grew up with them."

"My parents have always been over-protective with me. Sometimes it's out of hand."

"Geez, they'd love hearing about this trip then."

"No doubt, especially my dad."

The run down the Amelia River to the Fernandina Harbor Marina took less than ten minutes. They tied up at the public docking facility and Jack paid the dock master. Hand in hand they strolled through the town of Fernandina Beach exploring the historic district with its Victorian houses and quaint boutiques. The pirate theme was everywhere.

Jack went into tour guide mode as they took in the sights. "Like I said, this was a pirate's den until the early 1800's. The deep water, and the fact that the local authorities were able to work out a tolerance arrangement with the high seas bandits, made it the perfect hideout. Nowadays, the town remembers the old pirates during the first weekend every May, by staging reenactments of the invasions, combining it with their annual shrimp festival. It draws crowds from all around."

"What would pirates have to do with shrimp?"

"Nothing really, but shrimp is a huge industry here. I'll take you over to the docks and maybe we can walk around on one of the shrimp boats. They catch about two million pounds of shrimp each year from this little town. The Fernandina shrimp fleet is considered one of the biggest sources for the sweetest white shrimp in the Atlantic."

Throughout the afternoon, they chatted about the history of the town, their families, and their plans. Talia was completely taken with his knowledge of the area and its history, as well as his sense of adventure and self-confidence. Jack, on the other hand, thought Talia was not only the prettiest girl he had ever met, but also extremely smart and self-assured, without being full of herself. As promised, they visited the shrimp docks and feasted on freshly caught shrimp at a ramshackle riverfront wholesaler, sitting at a shabby wooden picnic table outside. As they were finishing their meal, Jack took on a worried look as his attention wandered toward the sky. Talia was busy sharing her concerns about starting school in an unfamiliar place when suddenly Jack stood from the table.

"What's the matter? You look like you've seen another ghost."

"Talia, we've got to get moving right away," Jack replied briskly as he stepped from between the bench and the table.

"Okay, but what's wrong?"

"The weather is what's wrong."

"It's beautiful. It's sunny, there's a nice breeze, the ......"

"The problem is the breeze. The wind picked up and the direction changed very suddenly. That's what made me look up to the sky. Those are vertical cumulus clouds developing and with that quick shift in wind direction, it means we're in for a big storm."

The two walked quickly toward the marina. Talia needed to take jogging steps to keep up. They were on *Bad Latitude* within five minutes. Once aboard, Jack turned on the NOAA (National Oceanographic and Atmospheric

Administration) weather band on the boat's radio, and grabbed a rolled up chart from below the helm.

"Do you want me to untie the boat yet Jack?"

Jack smiled as he looked up. "The term is *cast off* you landlubber," he teased. "Hang on just a minute 'til I check these charts. I want to see how we can get home through the Intracoastal Waterway and avoid going offshore."

"Why wouldn't we go the way we came?"

"If we run offshore, the seas are going to turn rough and there will be nowhere to go in case of trouble. The Intracoastal might take longer but it won't be nearly as treacherous. If things get really bad, we can at least beach the boat. We need to get underway, but we have to plot our course first."

"This sounds scary," said Talia.

"There's nothing to worry about. Cap'n Jack has it all under control."

At that moment, the electronic monotone voice from the oceanographic institute's weather reporter sounded over the radio - "*There is a small craft advisory in effect for the areas between St Mary's Georgia and Flagler Beach Florida - Winds are expected at twenty five to thirty knots with gusts up to forty - Sea swells ten to twelve feet - Heavy rain likely at times with a mix of hail – Dangerous lightning is possible......*"

Jack punched the keys on the GPS unit, logging waypoints to follow and finally started the engine. He carefully folded the chart and stowed it in the glove box at the helm. After a thoughtful pause, he reached into the storage box and removed two hooded raincoats, two life jackets, and two pair of clear safety glasses. Once the gear was ready, he moved to the bow, retrieved the anchor from the storage locker, and carefully checked to make sure there were no tangles in the line. He returned the anchor to the locker but left the rope coiled on the deck. It was still sunny and mild.

"You can cast off now matey," said Jack.

Talia looked nervous as she removed the spring line and tossed it upward onto the pier.

"If I wasn't scared before, I am now." Talia had put up a brave front but the strain was beginning to show. Jack's preparations made it appear that certain trouble was ahead. "Why did you get all of this stuff out anyway? Is it going to be that bad?"

"It's okay. I'm just taking precautions. Moving through heavy rain, in a mostly open boat like this, stings when it hits your skin. I took the life jackets out in case it gets really choppy."

"You mean there's a chance we could sink?"

"No, not at all. If it gets really rough, we're gonna put them on. Just because the boat won't sink doesn't mean one of us couldn't fall overboard. I've been in some nasty storms before and it doesn't make sense to wait for an emergency and then have to scramble around in bad weather collecting the gear," replied Jack matter-of-factly.

"What about the anchor? What's that for?"

"If we have to get to the riverbank, I want be able to anchor up in a hurry instead of dealing with a tangled mess in the middle of a heavy chop and a driving rain."

"Whatever you say Cap'n." Talia calmed down and smiled.

"What are you smiling about?"

Talia stared into his eyes. "Nothing that you would understand."

Jack shrugged absently and reached for the cell phone. He called Pop to let him know where they were and what their headings would be. They would keep their radios tuned to the same frequency and communicate back and forth. It would help

Pop keep track of their progress and location at all times, while keeping emergency help just a phone call away.

Bad Latitude sliced through the waters at full speed past Crane Island, Amelia City, and through the South Amelia River. The tricky part of the trip was crossing behind Nassau Sound into Sawpit Creek. There were several shallows shown on the charts, giving Jack no choice but to slow considerably. The winds were picking up and the skies were turning the color of charcoal. He had hoped to reach the Tolomato River before the storm caught them. Navigating the shallows and crossing Chicopit Bay in a windy downpour would be tricky and dangerous. They had been underway for nearly an hour and Jack had pushed the boat as hard as he dared for as long as he could. Finally, he throttled back to near idle and turned toward Talia.

"Let me help you with your raincoat and life jacket. It's going to get real rough real quick."

Talia's fingers trembled slightly as she worked to fasten the straps. The blackness had descended upon them and the winds were gusting furiously. A curtain of water was advancing on them from the northeast and would pounding away at them within minutes.

15

Life Jackets

Pop paced the workshop. It had been two hours since Jack had explained his predicament and more than thirty minutes since their last radio contact. The wind and rain was intense and the noise from the storm was deafening, sounding, at times, as if rocks were being thrown against the side of the building. Considering the racket, Pop assumed that Jack couldn't hear the radio or was, perhaps, preoccupied with handling the boat in the treacherous conditions.

Pop had no doubt that *Bad Latitude* could withstand difficult elements and knew Jack was highly skilled at the helm. His biggest worry was lightning and, so far, there had been none. He hoped they had reached the Tolomato River where deeper water would eliminate at least one obstacle. Checking his watch, he returned to the radio for another attempt at raising Jack.

While taking his seat, the door burst open with a gust of wind driven rain. Standing in the open doorway was Nan in her hooded rain slicker. After slamming the door closed with her foot, she walked to the workbench where Pop was stationed at the two-way. As if by magic, she produced a large cup of coffee from below the pale blue slicker and put it down on the bench next to his elbow.

"So I assume that you haven't heard from him," Nan said conversationally.

"Not for about thirty, maybe thirty five minutes."

"Don't worry. He knows what he's doing. He had a great teacher. This will clear up soon and he'll be docking up in a little while," said Nan as she draped a soaking wet arm across Pop's shoulder.

Pop was upset over more than the storm and the radio problem.

Acting the part of mind reader, Nan continued. "You weren't wrong telling him the island was off limits. You never tolerated disrespect from your boys and shouldn't from him."

"Yeah, I know, but he was so close and now he thinks his dream just went bust."

"He won't go there now that you told him not to."

"I know. Maybe I was too harsh."

"You were, but you had to get his attention. He was obsessed with that treasure and nothing else in the whole world seemed to matter to that kid. Give it a day or two and maybe you guys can reach an agreement."

"What kind of agreement?"

"Tell him to hurry up and get over there to claim that gold before he has to travel home," said Nan.

"You gotta be kiddin' me. I don't believe it. Now you're tellin' me it's okay if he goes out there again at night chasin' after that gold with spooks or whatever else is out there. What'd you put in your coffee today?" Pop stood up, smiling, and shaking his head.

"Hey, I'm not going to stand back and watch someone's dreams shattered, especially Jack's. I always backed you when you had some dream to chase, same with the boys. Why would I let something like a little old skeleton coming to life, grabbing my grandson and trying to kill him make me worry? After forty two years with you, what could possibly scare me?"

Pop rubbed the back of his neck and chuckled. "Guess I've been outmaneuvered. You always know which buttons to push, I'll give you that. You're right. Jack and I will talk and get everything worked out."

"Looks like the rain and wind is letting up a bit now. You can see the sun breaking through way up river and the worst seems to be over. I'm going back to the house to let you pace in peace."

Pop laughed again, gave Nan a peck on the cheek, and turned toward his workbench. He reached for his coffee and radio handset and settled in with the mixed sense of hope and relief.

While Pop and Nan were having their chat, and Jack and Talia were battling the storm in *Bad Latitude*, Kai and Val were in the middle of a heated discussion.

"You guys have been best friends for almost ten years. He was being a jerk because he had his dream right there in his hands and it was just snatched away. You need to cut him some slack and make things right before he goes back home," lectured Val.

Kai crossed his arms over his chest defiantly. "So why can't he be the one to try to patch things up?"

"He did! How many times do you want him to apologize? Talia and Jack are leaving in a week or so and after that, you're not going to see him for almost a year. Do you want to lose your best friend over something stupid like this?"

"You're right, I guess. I'm carryin' it too far. I just get sick of always havin' to do everything his way. I'm not sayin' he's a bad guy. It's just, I don't know, he's like *Mr. Perfect* or somethin'." Kai's stubborn display was collapsing fast.

"You're gonna get mad at me, but I'm saying what needs to be said. I think you're jealous. He has everything going for him and can do almost anything he wants. What you're forgetting is, he was willing to let you in on the secret, and splitting the treasure with you fifty-fifty. You can't say he's greedy. He's always been generous and kind hearted. He's hardly ever rude and doesn't go around acting like his family's loaded, which they are. Did you ever think of any of that? How many people do you know like that?" argued Val.

"Alright, you've made your point. I'll call over there later n' see what's up."

"Call now. Maybe we can all hang out tonight."

"Geez girl, you don't know when to quit."

"Call him."

Kai went to the phone and dialed the number. Nan answered on the first ring.

"Hi Nan, hope I'm not botherin' you or anything."

"No Kai, you're never a bother. I'm just waiting for a call, that's all."

"Okay, well, can you ask Jack to give me holler after you get your call? I'm at Val's."

"I'm actually waiting to hear from Jack."

"Is everything alright?" asked Kai.

"He and Talia took the boat up to Fernandina today and got caught in the storm on their way back. Pop hasn't been able to reach them on the radio for about an hour. I'm sure they're fine. The weather probably knocked out the radio. It's been a little tense around here but I'm sure it'll be okay."

Kai tried to sound unfazed. "Yeah, they're fine. They probably docked up somewhere to wait it out. You'll hear from him soon. He knows what he's doin' out there. At least the wind and rain is finally lettin' up."

"You're right Kai. They'll be fine. I'll have Jack call you as soon as he gets back."

Val was fidgeting, trying to figure out what was going on. When Kai hung up, she unloaded with a barrage of questions. Kai told her about the boat trip and suggested they go over to Pop's, just in case their help was needed. Val was out the door ahead of Kai.

Kai was right with his assumption that Jack and Talia had tied up to ride out the storm. When the radio shorted out, traveling further became too risky and they pulled alongside a private dock and tied off the spring and stern lines. Jack had cinched a blue tarp to the cleats at the stern, hooking it to the back rail of the T-top, creating a shelter from the driving rain. There they spent more than an hour huddled together behind the helm. The cell phone remained tucked away in a waterproof bag. The phone's battery was low and he didn't want to plug it into the helm power outlet during the storm and risk short-circuiting it. He would wait to get in touch with Pop as soon as the weather cleared, though he knew Pop and Nan would be worried.

When the storm let up, Jack checked his chart again comparing it with the waypoints entered into the GPS device. There was a good chance they wouldn't make it home before dark. When the tarp was removed, Jack started the engine and began wrapping up the ropes from the dock's pilings. His back and legs felt cramped from stooping so long below the cover.

"Hey, this is a private dock you know," came a voice from overhead.

"Uh, sorry. We got caught in the wind and rain and thought it would be safer to stop and rig up some shelter. My boat didn't bang into anything and we never went onto your dock or near your boat," explained Jack nervously.

The owner smiled from under his golf umbrella. "I'm just giving y'all a hard time. We were watching you kids during the worst of it, but there wasn't much we could do. My wife sent me out here to see if we could get y'all anything, or maybe fix y'all some supper."

Jack relaxed and returned the smile. "I appreciate the offer and the use of your dock, but we need to get moving. My grandparents are probably worried. We still have a two hour ride and my radio is out of commission."

"Do you want to use our phone and call them?"

"Thanks anyway, I have a cell phone. I'll call when the rain lets up a little more."

"No problem kids. Have a safe trip. By the way, that was very smart tying up instead of trying to travel through that mess. You've got a good head on your shoulders. Sure you don't want to call before you leave, you know, just to make sure you can get through?"

"Yeah, that's probably not a bad idea. Let me give it a shot."

The phone kept coming up with a *no service* message. After several attempts, Jack decided to give the man the number for his grandparents so he could call to let them know where they were and that all was fine.

The man looked at the scribbled note and back to Jack. "You've got to be kidding me. You're Rackham's grandson? Why we've been friends for years. He's got that big Donzi center console that's all rigged up. Worst fisherman I ever saw. I'll run in and call right now. It won't take but a minute. Y'all can come inside if you want to. It's up to you.

Jack thanked the man again but chose to wait with the motor running.

Within a few minutes, the man scurried back. "He's relieved to hear you kids are okay and said to tell you to be careful the rest of the way. Everybody's waiting for you, whatever that means. Hey, least I got me an invite for a fishing trip next week. That old boy can't catch nothin' but he's got some nice set up. Y'all be careful now."

With another round of smiles, Jack and Talia shoved off, moving down river toward home. The two-hour ride was relaxing and uneventful and they arrived at the boathouse under a canopy of brilliant stars. Talia was somewhat disappointed that their adventure was over. She would be leaving in six days for her new home.

Approaching the boathouse, they could see the tiki torches lit along the walkway and on the rooftop deck. It looked like a party was going on and Talia squinted through the darkness trying to see. She was excited when she spied Val and Kai leaning together against the upper railing.

With Pop and Kai pitching in, it took less than ten minutes to get *Bad Latitude* cleaned up and tucked away. The boys spent a couple of awkward minutes alone outside the boathouse, each apologizing to one another. Finally, Jack's rumbling stomach took over and they headed inside for a dinner of stuffed shells and meatballs. Being one of Kai's favorites, he seated himself at the table ahead of the others with eager anticipation. It didn't matter that he had eaten only a few hours earlier. Talia, now completely comfortable in the company of Jack's grandparents, kept pace with the guys, gobbling down several of the cheese stuffed pasta shapes along with three of Nan's meatballs.

Kai and the girls lingered at the house for a little while after dinner before leaving for the night. Jack was exhausted and the need for sleep was overwhelming. He started toward the boathouse apartment just before midnight. Walking through the door at the top of the stairs, he was startled to find Pop sitting in the recliner with an unlit cigar clamped between his teeth.

"Didn't mean to make you jump outta your skin like that, but I thought we needed to clear the air about a few things," Pop began.

"It's okay Pop, like I said; I was out of line and shouldn't have…"

"That's all over and done with now. Your apology squared all of that away already. I wanted to get your attention but think I went a bit too far," Pop interrupted. "Now hear me out. Nan and I talked it over. We want you to give that treasure hunt one more shot. You need to get back to that island soon, while the timing of the tide still works."

Jack couldn't believe it and broke into a grin. "You're serious about this?"

"Of course I'm serious. Have you ever known me to kid around?"

"You kid around all the time."

"Yeah, well, right now anyway, I'm not kiddin'."

"It's going to turn out different this time. I'm coming back with the gold."

"I have no doubt you will. Now it's time for this old boy to turn in," said Pop as he hauled himself out of the chair.

"Maybe I'll take the long way back to the house and sneak a few puffs on this mighty fine Montecristo."

No longer tired, Jack sat in the recliner restlessly daydreaming about his return to Rattlesnake Island.

Kai

16

Black Eyes and Stitches

Kai was stoked as he made his way out to test ride the new board that his parents were convinced would be a top seller at their surf shop. The winds were favorable for an early morning start and he tucked the lightweight board under his arm and began the brisk walk toward the beach. Normally he would cut through the neighbor's property, but they were in town for the week so he took the legal path that everyone else used. His timing couldn't have been worse. He never noticed the beat up van with ladders on the roof slowly following his progress.

As he reached the public access ramp, the white van picked up speed and made a wild turn to cut him off. In the process, the front fender of the van clipped the new surfboard, breaking it in half, knocking Kai off balance and into the dune next to the pathway. Before he could react, the two thugs,

Willie and Billy were on top of him and Kai felt an explosion of pain in the middle of his face.

"We warned you that we was gonna git you sooner or later surfer creep," hollered one of the twins, his fists moving piston-like, smashing an already dazed Kai in the side of the head three more times.

The wind rushed out of him as he was kicked in the side and stomach by the twin standing above. He pulled his knees toward his chest to protect against another crushing blow while trying to shield his face and head with his arm. There was no way to fight back. As he twisted helplessly in the sand, the first attacker returned with a full bucket of paint, raising it two-handed above his head, intent on cracking Kai's skull. Everything went black as another kick landed just below his chin.

Eric was wading into the water with his own board when he saw the twin's van cut in front of his friend. Everyone knew about the feud between Kai and Willie and Billy and Eric, recognizing trouble when he saw it, abandoned his own surfboard in the white foam and ran toward the van to even the odds.

Fortunately, for Kai, Eric was able to knock Willie down with a powerful tackle an instant before the bucket came crashing down. Billy, startled to see the bulked up Eric, tried to make a run for it. He was too slow for the future Gator football star. Billy's left arm snapped as he slammed into the van's solid doorframe while Willie, sure that his ribs were broken, struggled into the driver's seat.

Eric knelt down, checking on Kai, when he heard the roar of the van's engine and turned in time to see Willie aiming the van in his direction. Thinking quickly, he grabbed the paint bucket and crashed it into the windshield of the oncoming vehicle, causing Willie to lose sight of his target and control of the van. Eric ran toward the driver's door but the twins escaped through the passenger's side. Ditching the vehicle, they fled up the ramp. With the threat eliminated, Eric gave up the chase, returning to help the badly injured Kai.

The first thing Kai saw was a teary-eyed Val. His head was throbbing and his mouth felt dry and swollen. It seemed to be stuffed with a mixture of sand and cotton. His body ached. Each breath was agonizing and, as he looked around the room, it began to spin, making him sick to his stomach. He could hear his father speaking in a loud and angry tone to someone outside the room, but it was impossible to follow the conversation. Finally fully awake, he asked Val to tell him what happened.

"You were jumped by Willie and Billy on your way to the beach. Your dad is filing a complaint with the Sheriff's Office and wants them picked up for assault," explained Val. "Eric saw the whole thing and rescued you from those slimy creeps. They ran off and left the van behind. Now the Sheriff is going to interview Eric so they can track them down and lock the two of them up," she finished.

As Val filled Kai in on the details that she knew, Jack and Talia plowed their way into the crowded hospital room. Jack was furious when he saw what the twins had done to his friend.

Once the noise from multiple conversations started escaping the room, a nurse entered and stood with her hands on her hips, her bulk filling the entire doorway. She looked as though she could take on the whole crowd, and ordered everyone out in a not so nice tone. Folding her arms across her chest, she scanned the room, daring anyone to give her a hard time. No one did, and everyone followed her orders, meekly retreating to the waiting area down the corridor.

"I can't believe what those animals did," fumed Jack. "Willie and Billy had better hope the Sheriff gets to them before I do."

Talia grabbed him by the hand and whispered as Val approached. "Jack, you have to calm down. You're not thinking straight. All you're going to do is get yourself in trouble trying to get even."

"You don't understand. That's my best friend in there. Kai can be off the wall sometimes, but he wouldn't hurt anybody. He didn't deserve to get beat up like that. I owe it to him to settle this score," he insisted angrily.

Pop arrived in time to hear the exchange between his grandson and Talia. He decided to step in before things spiraled out of control.

"Jackson, you need to listen to the good advice comin' from your friend here. Let the Sheriff do his job. Those two will be caught and they're gonna do some serious jail time. For now, just calm down and be thankful that Kai's gonna be okay."

"I know you're right, but they should have gone after me, not Kai. I'm the one that dumped the hot sauce in their faces a few weeks ago."

Pop patted Jack on the shoulder. "Let it go and see what happens. Kai's dad says they're keeping him overnight for observation and he'll be as good as new in a couple of days. If it makes you feel any better, it sounds like Eric did a number on both of 'em. Tell Kai you'll see him tomorrow and let him get some rest. C'mon, you guys can catch a ride with me."

Jack and Talia managed to sneak past the guard dog nurse to wish their friend well, promising they would see him later. Talia accepted the offer of a ride from Pop while Val chose to stay with Kai and his parents. As they left the hospital, the Sheriff's Deputy ushered Eric into a small room near the nurse's station to get his version of what happened.

After dropping Talia off, Pop and Jack stopped at the South Beach Grill for a late lunch of blackened fish tacos. Sitting at an ocean-side table, Pop tried to get Jack's mind off the senseless beating, returning to the topic of the treasure hunt and the best options for retrieving the gold. There was some doubt in Jack's mind whether or not Kai would be in any kind of shape to help. He was anxious to complete the quest before leaving for Pennsylvania, but didn't want to proceed without his friend.

"Give it a day or two and see how he feels," was Pop's advice. "He's young and strong. The doc said nothin' was broken, so he's probably just gonna be sore. Worst case scenario, you might hafta take the old geezer along for the heavy liftin' after all."

Jack laughed at that. "You could probably haul all three of those bags yourself without breakin' a sweat."

Kai was released early the next morning and, other than having two black eyes, half a dozen stitches, a thumping headache and a few bumps and bruises, there were no complications. Willie and Billy had been caught the night before, trying to hide in a shed behind their house, and spent the night in jail. The Sheriff charged both with assault, based on Eric's eyewitness account.

Jack walked into Kai's house minutes after Kai's arrival.

"Geez Rackham, it's a wonder you weren't on the freakin' porch waitin' like some Girl Scout sellin' Thin Mints," grumbled Kai as he entered the room.

"I'm just checking to make sure this whole thing wasn't a set up. I figured maybe you would do anything to get out of digging."

"There ain't enough gold in that hole to make me dig today. I think I'll be okay by tomorrow though. Hey, I thought Pop said the island was off-limits."

"He changed his mind, so everything's cool. If you're up for it, we'll go tomorrow night. If not, no big deal. I'll get a new partner and work out an eighty twenty split," Jack teased.

"Ain't *you* the sympathetic one?"

"That's me. Hey did you hear they caught those creeps last night tryin' to hide in plastic trash bags in a shed?"

"Figures they'd try to imitate trash."

"Seriously," Jack continued, "tomorrow is best as long as you're up to it. Talia leaves in a few days and I'm outta here myself in six. If we can't do it tomorrow, it'll have to be three days from now and that's cutting it way too close."

"Listen jerk weed. Just relax. I toldja I'd be ready, so plan on tomorrow night. Now, hit the road so I can get some rest and hand me that ice pack before you go."

Jack was excited. Kai was in better shape than anyone could have expected. The bullies were locked up for the time being and the treasure hunt was on again full speed ahead. Things were falling into place. He stopped at the surf shop to buy some clothes before meeting up with Talia. Their time together was running short and he wanted to make the most of it. He didn't know when, or if, they would see each other once she left town.

After choosing a black Quiksilver shirt and a pair of cargo shorts, Jack walked along the beach toward home. He noticed a man waving his metal detector in a back and forth motion over the sand, close to the edge where the low tide surged. The man wore brightly colored plaid shorts that reached his knees and black socks pulled up tight, just below the shorts. A clashing orange and brown striped short-sleeved shirt, partially buttoned, stretched over the man's ample belly. A baby blue Tar Heels hat completed the ensemble. Jack laughed to himself about the many times his father had threatened to buy a metal detector for the same purpose. He was grateful that his dad had a better sense of style than the guy on the beach. Watching the nickel collector work his way along the sand, he thought about the gold waiting for him on the island and was suddenly struck with an idea and picked up his pace anxious to discuss his new plan with Pop.

Approaching the back of the main house, Jack saw that the deck boat was out of its hoist. He assumed Pop and Nan had taken a boat ride, maybe anchoring off one of the small beaches near the Matanzas Inlet for a beachside cookout. Since no one was home, he fixed himself two shrimp salad sandwiches and carried them out to the boathouse. He had no idea that his grandparents were on a scouting mission to Rattlesnake Island.

Pretending to be nature photographers and wearing high rubber boots over their shoes Pop and Nan trudged through the high grass across the island. First, they inspected the vicinity where the treasure was buried, then focused their attention on the row of palmettos where Pop had heard the movement and strange noises a week earlier. As they edged their way along the thicket, Nan noticed several branches snapped off and signs of flattened grass. Pop separated a section of heavy brush, shimmied sideways through the dense foliage, and climbed past the line of palmetto and sticker bushes. Fifteen feet inside the hedgerow, he stopped and began taking photos with one of Nan's digital cameras. He was stunned with what he uncovered.

Just beyond the thick brush was a small clearing. Within the clearing were several patches of loose soil where the marsh grass was missing or partially covered by dirt. He knew that this was not an area where the boys had been searching. The patches were larger than anything a small animal would cause searching for grubs or rodents. They looked to be the size of small graves, with a particular symmetry, and dug by hand rather than with tools. Kneeling next to the largest uprooted spot, Pop closely inspected and photographed the telltale marks resembling something made by a small rake. Spreading the fingers of his own large hand across the markings, he noted that the distance between the lines in the patterns closely matched the spacing between his own fingers. Prodding further, he determined the soils were still loose for the entire depth of the three-foot long stick he was using as a probe. Whatever had created the markings could be lying somewhere beneath the sand and soil. There was no doubt in Pop's mind that this was part of the ancient burial ground and something had escaped the unmarked grave. The question nagging at him was whether the corpse had returned to its grave or had it escaped, hidden elsewhere, waiting for the boys to return.

Pop stood, shut the power to the camera off, and walked toward the thicket to rejoin Nan. As he took his first steps through the brush, he failed to notice the rhythmic upward movement of the disturbed earth where he had knelt moments before. Had he turned to take one last look, he would have seen the pulsing motion of the soils. The fresh mound of dirt was breathing and rotted fingers broke through to the surface.

17

The Carriage Ride

Talia checked her hair and make up one last time as she waited for Jack to arrive. There were clothes scattered all across the bed, outfits that hadn't quite made the grade. She chose a very short brightly colored sundress and a pair of dainty white sandals. Finally, the doorbell rang and she hurried through the living room to greet him.

Hand in hand, they sauntered through the ancient city for, what could be, the last time together. She would be leaving in a few of days to begin school in a new city.

Their first stop was a visit to Flagler College. Talia, having fallen in love with the area, was seriously thinking of attending the school, wanting to pursue a major in Journalism and Creative Writing. Flagler was a four-year liberal arts college that offered both. Jack joked that he might be interested in Flagler as well, since the student ratio was three to one, girls to guys. The campus, situated in the center of St. Augustine, had been built originally as the very luxurious Ponce de Leon Hotel by Henry Flagler in 1883. The sculptures, architecture, and original artwork, including the stained glass circular windows, produced by Tiffany's of New York, only added to the campus charm. The proximity to miles of beautiful white sandy beaches was a fringe benefit that came at no extra cost.

After a late lunch at one of the many restaurants that offered outdoor seating, they casually explored the interior of *Castillo de San Marcos*. The visit included access to the guardrooms, the interior drawbridge, watchtowers and plaza. It was on the fortress seawall where they had first seen one another, and the site of their very first kiss, but would be the first time they had toured the site's interior together. After leaving the ancient stronghold, they meandered through town, occasionally stopping along the way to buy special gifts to take home to their families.

As the sun began to set, Jack suggested that a quiet carriage ride would be a relaxing way to end the day. There were several carriages to choose from and they settled on one being drawn by a huge brown horse and driven by a pleasant looking blonde lady.

"We would like to take the carriage tour, but prefer to skip the stories about the history and such, if you don't mind," said Jack very politely.

The carriage drivers were always very informative, describing the fine points and history of the old city. It was usually one of the more memorable highlights for many of the tourists visiting the town. For this ride, Jack preferred to spend his time quietly with Talia, without the interruption of the driver's narrative. The carriage driver took no offense to the request, realizing they were not the typical out of town guests.

"I don't mind at all. It might be a nice change of pace for me," the driver smiled. "My name is Elayne, by the way."

"Well, I appreciate that Elayne. I know you have a set route and a scheduled timetable that you have to stick to, so I won't ask you to go slower or take different streets. Can we hire you for back-to-back rides through town and maybe pause at a few spots where I can tell a few tales of my own?" he asked.

"I can handle that. Sometimes it's nice to get a break from the history lessons. Maybe I can learn something from your stories, that is, if you don't mind me listening. I promise I'll only listen when we stop," she added. "I'll have to tie up for a few minutes once when we get back to the waterfront so Dumpy here can get a drink. We have to abide by very strict rules for the care of our horses."

Jack helped Talia into the coach and they were off on their laid-back ride through the ancient city. At the first turn, just past the old fort and the *Huguenot Cemetery*, their driver stopped, giving him the chance to rush into a corner sandwich shop to buy three large sweet teas. Elayne was grateful for the refreshing beverage. It was nearly dark as the tour restarted.

Even Dumpy seemed to understand that it was a ride not to be rushed and he clip-clopped through the quiet streets as if it was the last fare of a long night. Fifteen minutes into the tour, Jack asked Elayne to pull to the curb as he pointed to an ornate house serving as one of St. Augustine's elegant bed and breakfast accommodations.

"Do you see those large windows with the circular tops across the front of that big house on the corner?" asked Jack. Talia nodded and rolled her eyes, knowing that a story was on the way. Elayne pulled back gently on the reins and shifted sideways in her seat. She wasn't about to be bashful about her eavesdropping and decided to do so comfortably.

"More than one hundred and fifty years ago this building was used as a funeral home. In its heyday, it was one of the few mortuaries where bodies were embalmed before burial. Can you guess the reason for the large windows?"

Talia's eyebrows arched. "Don't tell me they did the embalming in front of the windows so people could watch."

"No, but you're close. Elayne, do you know?"

"I think so, but let's hear your version of the story."

Jack continued. "Because the mortician was able to preserve the bodies using the newfangled method, he displayed his handiwork right there in those windows. Once the body was prepared, it was dressed up real nice, make up was applied, and the corpse was placed in a propped-up casket with the lid removed. It was left to stand, facing the street, for as long as two whole weeks. Neighbors would gather to pay their respects and admire the undertaker's artistry.

The funeral director always set the burial date in order to get the maximum use out of his clients. It was an early form of advertising, paid for by allowing the family a discount for his services, based on the number of days that the stiff remained, uh…. useful."

Talia giggled. "Did they post a sign below the dead people saying *This could be you?*"

Elayne laughed at that, then added, "They did put price tags at the bottom of the, uhm… displays. Helped to hide the bare feet. Shoes didn't get wasted back in those days. If someone had been buried with their boots on, you'd best believe they'd have been dug up by morning and left in the box with just their naked little toes poking up."

"When did the undertaker decide on the burial date?" asked Talia.

David Ebright

"Once the fingers started turning black and curling away from the body," answered Jack.

"That's so gross! You're making that up!"

Elayne turned a little more to her right to face Talia. "Sorry kid. He's telling the truth, but forgot to mention that if the undertaker didn't get the embalming just right, purplish patches would spread across the dead guy's face and then the little show was over. It was sorta like fruit going bad, without the little flies."

Talia felt her stomach churn slightly as she buried her face in the side of Jack's chest. She was trying to push the picture of a decomposing corpse out of her mind.

Jack winked at Elayne before they moved away from the curb. "The fly thing was a nice touch. I'll have to remember to include it next time."

They continued along, Jack's arm draped over Talia's shoulders, sipping sweet tea and gazing at the attractions in the twilight. From time to time, Jack would comment about points of interest or throw in a scary tale, but mostly they relaxed and enjoyed their time together. They pulled to the curb in front of the harbor for Dumpy's snack and water. There was a cute young girl waiting at the curb and she reached for the bridle to steady the horse as Elayne climbed from the seat. "Ryane, these folks are going for a second ride so we can't dilly dally."

"Great, I'll empty Dumpy's potty bag next time around," said Ryane.

"You know the rules; the bag gets emptied after every trip, no matter what."

"Geez, I've got one semester left 'til I get my degree, and I end up with a summer job emptying horse poop," the girl whined. "This job really stinks. Why don't you stop feeding him so much?"

"Ry, just empty the bag so we can get going."

"You got it Miss Laynie, but I'm putting Kaopectate in his feed from now on. This horse isn't normal."

Elayne laughed. "You never wondered how this horse got his name?"

With their driver occupied and out of earshot for a few minutes, Talia ventured forward with a question of her own. "Jack, we've known each other for almost three months now and we really like each other. How come you only kissed me that one time?" she felt her face redden as she asked, unsure of the response she might get.

Jack paused before turning to look her in the eyes. His words were calculated and direct. "I'm nuts about you and have been since the day we met. The problem is, you're leaving soon. We probably won't see each other again, unless you come back here next summer. I've never had a girlfriend, but it wouldn't be fair, for either of us, to expect to be some kind of long distance couple. That doesn't mean we can't be long distance friends and stay in touch by phone or email and who knows how things would turn out later? I just wouldn't want to build up some kind of crazy hopes or expectations for either of us. That wouldn't be fair."

"I see your point and it makes sense. What if we could see each other more often?"

"That would be great, but three thousand miles is a pretty huge distance to cover for a weekend or holiday."

"I told you, we were leaving Los Angeles. My dad took a job with a new company."

"Yeah, I know that, but how does it change anything?"

"Well, my parents sent me some pictures of our new house last week and gave me the address and the phone number so I could give them to you. Our new house is in Pennsylvania," Talia added with a huge smile.

Jack was caught off guard. "Pennsylvania is a big state. I live near Harrisburg. Where, exactly, are you moving?"

"Have you ever heard of Downingtown? It's about forty five minutes outside of Philadelphia."

"This has to be some kind of joke."

"No, really, we've moved to Downingtown."

"That's only ninety minutes from my house. My grandparents moved here from Downingtown and it's the town where my dad and uncle grew up. They graduated from the same school that you'll probably go to."

"It's a beautiful area, lots of hills and trees, and it's real close to the Amish farms, Valley Forge, and the city. I spent a lot of time online checking things out and it looks like a fun place to live. Best of all, we'll be close enough to see each other."

"This is awesome. I can't believe it. I'll be getting my license in about four weeks so we can visit anytime we're off from school."

"I was worried about telling you, but Nan was right."

"Nan knew about this?"

"I told her last week, but I begged her not to say anything. I wanted to see for myself how you would react."

"So what did she say? She must have been happy. Nan likes you a lot."

"You're right. She was really happy and predicted that you would be excited."

"Nan knows me better than almost anyone."

Elayne returned to the carriage to start the second tour. The ride was spent holding hands and making plans for future visits together. Ryane met them once again as they arrived at the final stop along the harbor. Jack thanked Elayne for the perfect ride and, still pumped from Talia's shocking good news, handed the driver an attention-getting tip, with an extra ten thrown in for Ryane.

They walked along the seawall that separated the city from the harbor, enjoying the quiet bustle of the town, the offshore movement of the boats and the sounds of acoustic guitars from nearby cafés. Finally, Jack explained to Talia that he still intended to retrieve the treasure from the island. He finished his gentle, but firm announcement, trying to make it clear that he would not be swayed. Talia sighed and shook her head as Jack prepared for another argument on the topic. It never happened.

"One of the things Nan warned me about was your stubbornness. She said it runs in the family, along with the strong desire for adventure. I guess that's to be expected from a family that comes from a bunch of pirates. I'm going to be worried until you're back safe, but I'm not going to be a drag about it like I was before. What's so appealing about you and your family is you're never dull. At home, I've always been treated like some porcelain doll and *that* is boring. So I guess I'll have to deal with it and hope it all works out."

"Well, that's a relief; I thought I'd be ruining our evening by telling you. Stubborn I'll admit to and I'm definitely looking forward to a life full of travel and adventure."

"I have no doubt about that," Talia laughed.

It was approaching midnight when they reached Talia's. They kissed goodnight and Jack moved on toward home.

18

Full Moon

Jack walked through the door into the boathouse apartment and found Pop napping in the recliner. Worried that something was wrong he shook him by the shoulder.

"Pop, wake up. Is everything Okay?"

"Huh? What? Yeah, everything's fine," answered Pop as leaned forward rubbing his face.

"Whaddya doing over here? Nan finally kick you out of the house?"

Pop chuckled. "Nah, didn't get the boot yet. I wanted to talk to you about the island and decided it was too important to wait. Nan and I were over there today nosin' around and found somethin' you need to know about."

"Nan was over there today?"

"Yeah. She wanted to see everything for herself. It's a good thing we made that trip."

"Does this mean the dig is off?"

"No. It means you need to make some strategy changes. Now the dig becomes a race. You're gonna have to grab n' go."

"So what did you find?"

"Remember those sounds and the movement from that line of palmettos just east of where you guys were diggin'?"

"Yeah, I remember. It was pretty scary." Jack replied.

Pop went on to describe what he had found behind the hedgerow and spent the next thirty minutes stressing the need for completing the recovery with great care and lots of speed.

"There's no doubt about it. Once you guys disturb the earth in those burial grounds, you'll wake the dead buried in that clearing and they'll leave their graves tryin' to stop you n' Kai from escapin'. If you decide not to follow through on this, you'll get no criticism from me." Pop winked. "On the other hand, it'd be one heckuva an adventure."

Jack didn't hesitate. "I still want to do it Pop. I know we can pull this off."

"You're gonna have to tell Kai about what we found out there n' give him a say in it. He might want to back out. It wouldn't be fair for him not to know about what might be waitin'."

"I'll talk to him about it first thing tomorrow. If he decides not to go, then what do I do?"

"See what he has to say, but I think he'll tell you he's still in." Pop stood up to leave. "I'd better turn in buddy, just in case you need me to pinch hit tomorrow night."

Jack flopped into the recliner vacated by his grandfather. He was grateful that Pop and Nan had checked things out. The extra warning couldn't hurt. After fifteen minutes, deep in thought, he stood and retrieved a notepad, pen and his battered map of the island with the location of the treasure clearly highlighted. Estimating the distance between the dig location and shoreline, he began to formulate a new plan for claiming the treasure while, hopefully, making a clean escape from whatever lurked behind the line of palmettos. It was a little past two when he fell asleep in the big chair.

At ten the next morning, Jack showed up at Kai's and explained the details of Pop's discovery in an uninterrupted narration. Kai, barely awake when Jack first arrived, sat at the kitchen table staring straight ahead. He had several angry looking bruises on the side of his face and a neat row of stitches on his cheek below one eye. After a couple of minutes of complete silence, Kai turned toward his friend.

"I'm feelin' much better. Thanks for askin' butthead."

"My bad. I got so caught up in what Pop told me, I never thought about asking how you were doing," Jack replied.

"Yeah, I know. I woulda been the same way. It's pretty sucky news if you ask me."

"I had to tell you about it. If you want out, I'll understand. If I get away with the gold, I'll still split it with you."

"Nah. If I don't help on the island, I ain't collectin' any of the money."

"Why not? You worked your rear end off out there for days and days alongside me in all that heat and humidity. You suck as a snake lookout but I couldn't blame you if you didn't want to go back, especially being all banged up like you are."

"I'm not that banged up. I look worse than I feel. There's still no way I'm bailin' now. You're gonna need all the help you can get."

The truth was, Kai felt worse than he looked but wasn't about to let Jack down.

"If you're in that's great. I think I have a plan….."

Kai interrupted. "Here we go again. Always with the plan. You knew I'd agree to this before you even got here."

"Yeah," Jack laughed. "I never had any doubt."

"Okay Einstein, so let's hear it from the beginnin'."

Jack explained it all; making a point this time to pause for Kai's input. The conversation went back and forth for well over an hour and by lunchtime, everything was fine-tuned. Kai agreed to meet at the boathouse just before dusk and Jack left for the hardware store.

The cashier peered suspiciously at the tall blonde kid standing at the register. His cart was piled with several coils of heavy rope along with three spotlights, and a couple rolls of duct tape. Curiosity finally got the better of her. "Either you're a very serious boy scout planning on practicing some knot tying or y'all got something y'all don't want getting away real bad," commented the clerk, the words coming in a slow-motion drawl.

"Nah, no boy scout. Just on an errand for my grandfather."

After arriving at the boathouse, Jack began assembling the gear needed for the final visit to Rattlesnake Island. He checked anchor lines, batteries, running lights, and spotlights, and made sure he had all the tools they might need. Finally satisfied, he took a quick dip in the pool, intending to rest up before Kai arrived. He had just started to towel off when Pop walked into the lanai.

"I guess you're all ready to go judgin' by the way your boat's all loaded up," said Pop.

"Yeah, I'm just waiting until dusk so we can get moving. Kai will be here in a little while."

"Well, there are a couple more curve balls you need to look out for, as if there weren't enough of 'em already." Pop continued. "First of all, there's a full moon tonight. That's not a good thing. Second......"

"Why is the full moon a big deal, other than visibility?" Jack interrupted.

"I'm gettin' to that if you would hold your horses a minute."

"Sorry. Proceed your Geezerness."

"And sorry you should be. A man my age can't be havin' his thoughts interrupted like that 'cause they might never come back. Now where was I?"

"Full moon tonight, not a good thing. Second... then I opened my yap."

Pop was ready to pounce with a jabbing comeback but thought better of it. He was trying to make a serious point.

"The full moon has always been a stimulant for supernatural activities. There are tons of legends and stories about strange happenings and sightings taking place around here when the moon is full, especially on the Matanzas. You've heard some of the more popular ones. Well, I suspect, and mind you I ain't some superstitious old coot yet, whatever is out there is gonna be more active and powerful tonight than it might be normally. I was lookin' up a story that I remember hearin' a few years ago. It seems some guys decided it would be a real kick to anchor up and camp on that island. I don't know if it was some kind of dare or what, but the next day the boat was still there but the guys were nowhere to be found. There were search teams sent out but after a couple of days, all they found was some gear but no other sign of the campers. Turns out there was a full moon the night it all went down and the locals, as usual, made a very big deal out of it, sayin' it was more proof that the island is haunted."

"Geez, this gets better and better. I can't wait to hear the rest."

"Well, the next point is just another maybe. Whatever is out there, it's like it has this job to protect that King's burial plot. I'm not sure why it, or maybe I should say they, wouldn't be buried closer to 'im. Whatever. Anyway, the next part of what I gotta tell you has me worried. When you guys get the goods and get off the island, what keeps whatever's out there from trackin' you down? I'm sure you could outrun it at first but you can't look over your shoulder the rest of your lives worried that some dead thing or things might grab you. Maybe you guys need to rethink this a little more. Frankly, I wish I'd done a better job researchin' it myself." Pop paused for a moment. "The other thing I need to point out is the river itself. It seems everyone thinks that's haunted too. That's why no one spends the night on their boats during a full moon. They say some parts of it turns red, like blood. Others say skulls bob to the surface and a green glowing fog forms. I know you'll be leavin' soon 'cause you're runnin' out of time, but maybe you should postpone this little adventure. I'll leave that up to you."

"Well, we can kick it around some and maybe can come up with something. I hate to get this close and chicken out."

"If you want to call it off, or want me to go, I'll understand," Pop suggested lamely as he turned and walked out of the lanai. He knew Jack's stubbornness would win out.

Kai arrived earlier than expected, walking past Pop as he was heading toward his shop.

"What's eatin' him? He barely said hello."

"He's worried 'cause it's a full moon n' stuff." Jack went on to retell the story, including the part about the missing campers and Pop's concern about the guys being tracked down by some dead thing.

Kai wasn't amused but didn't want to call off their trip. After a few minutes of silence, he began to grin. His grin turned to a smile. The smile turned to laughter. Jack stared at him like he had somehow lost his mind. Kai finally spoke up. "Rackham, I think I've got an idea that solves part of our problem."

"And what, my fuzzy friend, would that be?"

Kai spent the next ten minutes explaining his brainy scheme. Jack's own smile grew as he heard the plan take shape, convinced that Kai was really onto something. It was agreed they would keep it to themselves. They would need Pop's help, but not until early the next morning.

After lounging around the pool for a couple of hours and eating several blackened shrimp prepared by Pop on his pride and joy stainless steel grill, the boys went through their checklist and equipment one last time. Sunset was fast approaching and, as in the past, they wanted to anchor as darkness fell.

Before leaving the dock, Jack approached Pop who was sitting alone on the deck above the boathouse, hiding out from Nan, nervously puffing away on another hand rolled cigar.

"Pop, we're ready to shove off and I think we have just the right plan to get the treasure off the island safely and solve a few other little details while we're at it," Jack explained excitedly.

Pop perked up and stood to face his grandson. "You want to let me in on this brainstorm?"

"Trust me Pop. It's almost foolproof. To pull it off, we need you to meet us at the municipal dock first thing in the morning. Kai had some good points earlier and I think it's all gonna work out. We're staying out on the water all night, in case we get chased. We don't want anything coming back here to the house. I can keep running the boat to stay ahead of whatever is out there, meet you in the morning, and get you to put the treasure in safe deposit boxes over at the bank. While you do that, we're going to plant a little diversion to change the scent and send whatever might chase us, if that actually happens, onto another trail."

"I like it. It sounds workable, still totally nuts and dangerous, but workable. What time do you want me at the dock?"

"How about seven? Maybe you could bring us coffee while you're at it," Jack kidded.

"Now you're pushin' your luck."

"Hopefully we can pull off the snatch n' grab and get off the island before we wake the dead guys up."

"I doubt it. You sure you don't want me to go?"

"Nah. We'll be fine.

After a tight squeeze on Pop's shoulder, Jack turned away and hurried down the steps to jump aboard *Bad Latitude*. Within a few minutes, he and Kai were running at full throttle toward Rattlesnake Island. Pop stood at the rail watching the running lights fade into the distance as the boys continued south down the Matanzas. When they finally disappeared, Pop abandoned the railing and headed toward the steps. He worried that maybe this time; the boys had taken on an impossible challenge. Knowing it would be a rare sleepless night, he headed to the kitchen to brew the first of many pots of very strong coffee. There was a fine line between adventure and recklessness. Pop thought maybe this time, the line had been crossed.

19

Gravediggers

"So waddya gonna buy with your share Jack?"

"I have no idea, hadn't even thought about it to tell you the truth. I guess it depends on what it ends up being worth. How about you? You got any big plans?"

"I was thinkin' about gettin' some wheels. Three months to go 'til I can drive," said Kai thoughtfully. "I guess you've already got just about everything you want."

"Yeah right. When Pop bought me the boat, my parents were all bugged out about it. They thought I was way too young for something that big and expensive. They said I wouldn't have any ambition if everything was handed to me."

"You gotta admit your parents had a point, but it looks like Pop won that argument."

Jack smiled. "He wins *every* argument, unless it's with Nan. Pop told me once that he lets Nan *think* she's winning but says he's really outsmarting her that way."

"Is that why nobody ever talks about that wooden boat he bought n' named after her? He's still tap dancin' around that one."

"When Pop called to tell me about that boat, Nan was in the background complaining and telling him to take it back. He kept saying he couldn't and whispered to me it was a good thing he paid cash instead of using a check. When he called the boat *Deb's Temper*, he thought she'd think it was funny and it would all blow over in a little while. Nan told me she did think it was funny and never minded *that* much, but figured if she acted kind of upset, he wouldn't go ahead and spend a bunch of money like that again without at least talking about it with her first."

"Well, they never seem to ever argue 'bout much of anything."

"Yeah, that's 'cause Pop has a theory. He always says, *You can be right or you can be happy.*"

Kai thought about that bit of philosophy and then smirked. "So I guess your Pop's always wrong 'cause he seems happy most of the time."

"I guess that's one way of looking at it."

"That's cool. Hey, somebody needs to keep your family in line. Guess Nan's the right choice for that job. So when you go back north, do you live in some kind of mansion like Pop's and have everything anybody could ever want?" Kai asked.

"Mansion? Are you nuts? I live in a nice house, but we don't have everything and my parents don't give me anything I want just because I ask for it. I've got jobs to do; my grades have to be good, all that kind of stuff. That's the deal for me to be able to come down here every summer."

"Really? I just assumed you were just some kid from a loaded family that got picked up from school in a Rolls." Kai was kidding around and Jack finally caught on.

"Actually, I ride to school in one of those big yellow things with wheels. They call them buses where I'm from," said Jack.

"Awright, so you're *normal*, big deal. So waddya gonna buy when we finally get the cha ching?"

"Probably the same as you. Some kind of car or truck. Maybe save as much as I can so I can travel later. I'm not sure, it still depends on how much we get I guess."

"Looked like it was worth plenty to me," said Kai. "Hey, maybe I'll buy Pop's house."

They were approaching the island at exactly the right time. It was light enough to see without being conspicuous. They hustled getting the anchors set and tools unloaded before Jack looped the end of a rope into the starboard cleat and carefully unraveled the line as he waded onto shore ahead of Kai. Once ashore, they pulled on their boots and started trudging toward the burial plot. Kai dragged the cooler along, instead of leaving it behind like before, while Jack carried a huge duffel bag filled with the coils of heavy rope.

The moon was full, as Pop had warned, but partially hidden by a low cloud cover. As they followed the GPS and advanced toward the treasure, Jack continued rolling out rope onto the ground. At the end of each coil, he would double knot a new length onto the end to extend the line as they made progress. He had thought about trying to tie it together before the trip but decided there was too much risk for getting it tangled. For now, they would move as silently as possible and prepare for the life or death race across the island that both thought was probable.

The island was quiet, almost too quiet, giving Jack the odd feeling that their presence was already known. Kai also worried that they were being watched, but pushed the feeling out of his mind, blaming it on his still pounding headache. He resisted the urge to shine the light anywhere other than where they were walking. Having to stop so often to tie the rope ends together added to the tension and the weight of the rope coils and the large cooler was taking its toll on both of them. They were finally within a couple of hundred feet of the long abandoned grave when they ran out of rope. Jack took it as a bad sign. He'd thought he had bought too much.

"So what do we do now?" whispered Kai.

"We can take a chance and leave the rope and come back tomorrow night with more, or we can wing it. The whole idea was to have a way to drag the bags out of here in a rush if we got chased by something. If we can get the bags over to here and into the cooler, we still have a shot. It's your call," Jack answered in a hushed tone. He was looking through the darkness in the direction of the palmettos.

"Let's do it. C'mon hurry up."

Moving quickly and taking less care for quiet, Jack and Kai rushed to the loose soils where they had come so close to the buried prize twice before. They dug furiously with only quick glances to check for snakes or other unwanted visitors. The end of the lifeline rope, still tied to the three bags, was found exactly where Jack had hidden it. The boys used it as a guide for a more direct dig, trying to avoid the buried skeleton of the ancient Indian King. Once they reached the halfway point, the noises began and a horrible stench filled the air.

Kai was the first to notice. "I think we got company comin'. You can even smell 'em."

"I hate to ever admit you're right, but you're right."

"Don't talk, just dig."

The sounds were getting closer but Jack and Kai were determined to win the race. Neither stopped digging, there was too much at stake. Suddenly, Kai jumped and let out a yelp, causing Jack to turn with his shovel raised, ready to strike. As his eyes adjusted, he saw a look of relief spread across Kai's face.

"Sorry, I just found a piece of our long lost buddy here," explained a jumpy and slightly embarrassed Kai as he held up the amputated hand of the Indian King.

"That means we're really close. Pop threw that back in the hole just after I escaped that night. It can't be more than a couple of feet now." Jack returned to digging.

"Good thing we bagged all of it and tied it last time. We'd never have a chance scramblin' around with that rotted old box."

Kai never noticed the ground moving at the back side of the grave as the long dead King was trying once more to punish the pair of intruders. The rustle from the palmettos was growing steadily louder and they could hear a crawling motion through the grasses followed by gasps for air mixed with low moans and cries. Still, they pressed on.

"Watch my back Kai," Jack nearly shouted. "I've got the top of the bags; make sure the dead guy doesn't grab me while I'll pull them loose."

Jack pulled as hard as he could on the rope securing the three bags. Kai dragged himself to the top of the dirt pile to grab the end of the rope so he could give Jack a hand. Finally, the bags were loose and Jack joined Kai. With a quick look around, both grabbed the line and heaved together, scraping the bags up the side of the collapsing bank of sand and soil. Jack was grinning. "So far, so good partner."

"We ain't done yet. This was probably the easy part. Somethin's headin' this way and we gotta go that way," Kai pointed as his heart pounded.

"Yeah, okay. Just catching my breath. We're gonna make it. Let's get these bags sealed up in the cooler so we can start dragging them to the boat. It'll probably be a bumpy ride so we gotta make sure it can't fly open." Jack was trying to act like all was under control but wasn't so sure that Kai was buying his act. Within a few minutes, the cooler was loaded and sealed with duct tape. It was heavy, barely manageable even with both boys lifting together.

"Should we take these boots off in case we gotta make a run for it?" asked Kai

"Yeah, that makes sense. We might not have time to pull them off if we get to the water…"

"Whaddya mean if?"

"You didn't let me finish. I was gonna say …. if we get to the water with something on our tails, and have to jump in the river. The boots will fill up and slow us down."

"They'll slow us down anyway if we have to run, so let's do somethin' even if it's wrong." Kai hurriedly pulled the boots off.

Side by side, they marched at a crisp pace toward *Bad Latitude,* struggling with the heavy ice chest supported awkwardly between them. They reached the abandoned rope and Jack knelt down to grab the end.

"Let's just carry the cooler as far as we can." Kai barely paused as he looked toward Jack, nearly pulling him off balance.

"You're right, let's get closer to shore."

"We better pick it up, the sounds are gettin' closer, and we have a ways to go."

The weight of the cooler slowed them down. Their arms ached from the digging and hauling. As they reached the last third of the hike, a slight breeze began to blow and shadowy moonlight broke through the moving clouds, illuminating the island. Jack, not relying only on the abandoned rope as his guide, checked the GPS once again. If they hurried, they could make it to the boat in less than five minutes. Kneeling next to the ice chest, he cut the rope, looped it through both cooler handles, and knotted it securely as Kai looked on with an amused expression.

"You wanna let me in on what you're doin' there?" asked Kai.

"It looks like we're gonna have to make a run for it real soon. We might be able to carry this heavy sucker for just a little while longer. Whatever was in the palmettos is closing in on us fast. It's a good thing we took the boots off." Jack finished tying the cooler handles and stood up.

"Do you think we can outrun 'em?"

"Doesn't matter. Just so I can outrun you," laughed Jack in a whisper.

"That's what we need, a worn out old joke. Let's get goin'. Why don't we run now?"

"I'm hopin' they think we don't know they're followin' us yet. If we start runnin' too soon, we might not make it."

Kai reached for the cooler's handle. "Well let's shut up n' giddyup."

Jack didn't tell Kai that he could already see the clearly defined silhouettes of at least four pursuers and that they had spread out, trying to surround and intercept the boys before they reached the water. He decided that the last hundred yards would have to be covered in a sprint and he and Kai would have no choice but to split up. His mind raced as he considered their next move. After a couple of minutes, Jack began explaining the adjusted plan to his friend.

"Kai, we have four dead guys coming at us from four directions and they're going to be on top of us real soon."

"Yeah, I saw 'em about ten minutes ago when the wind started blowin'," whispered Kai.

"Thanks for telling me."

"I figured you already saw 'em."

"We're gonna have to split up to get to the water. There's a gap right now, but it's closing fast. When I say go, run as hard as you can to the boat and get the engine started and the bow anchor pulled up. We can cut the stern line if we have to. I'm gonna to stop here and shorten the rope one more time to make it easier to drag. Catch your breath and get ready, you only have a couple of minutes."

"Why we splittin' up? We can both drag the cooler while we run."

"We won't make it without a diversion so we're definitely gonna have to tow the cooler outta here with the boat. That's why I'm shortening the rope. If there's too much slack in it, the rope or cooler might break. You get to the boat and I'll make them chase me. As soon as you're ready, turn on the stern light. That will be my signal that you're ready and I'll run for the boat."

Kai took a couple of deep breaths. "Awright but I don't like it. Say when."

"Okay. Everything's as tight as it's gonna get. Ready?"

"Ready."

"Go for it!"

Kai sprinted toward *Bad Latitude*. Jack stood his ground a few moments longer to see how the guards would react. It seemed the element of surprise was working in Kai's favor and Jack ran on an angle toward the shape closest to Kai in an effort to distract it. The guard changed direction as soon as Jack got closer, temporarily ignoring Kai, while the other three picked up speed and converged, away from the water. Kai made it to the river and waded to the boat. The wind began howling wildly and the island took on a pale green yellow glow. A new sound followed, something from another world. It was the sound of the dead.

Jack zigzagged his way through the waist-deep grass. Finally, he could see that the stern light was on. He realized he was being forced into a trap by three of the skeletal monsters. The fourth was advancing on the ice chest filled with the treasure. It suddenly seemed his plan was about to fail. Jack ran toward the gold, trying to tempt the other guard into joining the chase. He looped behind, only an arm's length away, causing the fourth sentry to abandon the cooler and join the pursuit. There was a narrow gap left between the old warriors and he needed to get through it quickly if he was going to survive. His lungs and muscles burned as he sprinted through the snake-infested grass. Looking again toward the river, he had less than twenty yards to cover before reaching the water and the safety of *Bad Latitude*. The stern light was on. The engine was running. There was no sign of Kai.

20

Calico Jack's Ghost Ship

Pop was at it again, pacing the floor of his shop and checking his watch every few minutes. He figured he should have heard from the boys at least half an hour earlier. Something must have gone wrong. This time he wished he had insisted on going, at least as back up. He knew Jack wanted to complete the task on his own, but how smart could it have been to let him take the risk? Clicking off the radio, he walked out to the boat dock. After jumping aboard *Laffin' Gaff*, he turned the radio on to the agreed channel. He reached toward the ignition switch and stopped, deciding to give the boys a few more minutes before disappointing them with, what might be a premature rescue run.

Jack was panicking. He had never known such fear, but there was no way he was leaving the island without Kai. He stopped ten feet short of the water's edge and began yelling for his friend. Turning to his left, he found himself facing a seven-foot corpse only a few feet away. The decomposed flesh was regenerating over the skeleton and an evil grin began forming on the monster's face. Behind Jack, two more guards moved in, closing the gap. Ignoring the safety that *Bad Latitude* offered, Jack moved away from the water. Fifteen feet. Twenty. Thirty feet from the edge. He was slide stepping sideways, twisting back and forth calling out for Kai, when he tripped over the taut line connecting the boat and the cooler and landed helplessly on his back. He stared upward as the rotting guard moved swiftly to pounce on the trapped teenager.

"Stick 'em up!" Kai's voice carried over the howling wind.

Jack rolled to his right, catching a glimpse of Kai standing a few feet away with the flare gun pointed at the attacker. The gun was shaking and Kai tightened his grip.

"Just shoot it!" yelled Jack as he jumped to his feet.

In that instant, Kai pulled the trigger and the flare was released, slamming a flaming projectile into the chest of the long dead guard. The skeleton disintegrated on impact and the boys ran, diving into the river on the dead run. Within seconds, they were out of the water and aboard the boat.

"Cut the stern line and hold on. They're already in the water!" screamed Jack above the ear piercing screams.

Kai cut the stern line, abandoning the anchor, just as the first guard reached its bony arm over the port side gunwale. Jack juiced the throttle forward, enough to escape its hold and gain some separation, but backed the engine down after putting only twenty feet between the boat and the dead guards.

"Whaddya doin'? Give it the gas!" Kai hollered.

"Sit tight. We're gonna be okay," Jack yelled back. "I need to keep steady pressure on the rope and drag the cooler. If we yank too fast or too hard, the cooler handles will break and we'll lose the treasure."

"I don't care about the treasure. Get us outta here now!"

Jack ignored him and instead took a slow and steady course west dragging the ice chest along at a gentle pace. It wasn't long before the cooler, still intact, could be seen sliding toward the riverbank.

"As soon as it splashes, we gotta start pulling the line into the boat. We gotta work fast."

"Just drag it behind the boat. They're still after us."

"Just pull! The cooler is taped shut but I can't drag it underwater for long. It's not completely watertight."

When the cooler hit the river Kai began pulling the rope. Jack left the helm, letting the engine run at a slow trolling pace, and joined Kai at the stern to lend a hand. He kept an eye out on the boat's direction as well the progress of the chasers, now several yards behind. Finally, they grabbed the handles of the cooler and dragged it onto the swim platform. Kai strapped the cooler down as Jack cut the ropes away and tossed them onto the deck. An exhausted Kai collapsed in one of the helm seats as Jack finally increased speed. They now had a wake behind them and their escape was complete. The boys grinned and high fived each other as Jack reached for the radio.

Pop had just lowered *Laffin' Gaff* into the water when his grandson's voice came over the airways.

"*Bad Latitude* calling the *Laffin' Gaff.* You out there Pop?"

"*Laffin' Gaff* here. Everything okay Jack?" was the relieved response.

"Everything's great. We did it!"

"Terrific! I'm proud of you guys. Call me on the cell phone so you can fill me in on all the details. I don't wanna talk over the radio."

"Okay Pop, give me a few minutes, I need to tighten up a few things here first."

Jack put the receiver in the holder attached to the radio and slowly turned toward Kai. "Stick 'em up? You actually yelled stick 'em up?"

"Awwww I knew I was gonna hear about that as soon as it was outta my mouth. I save your rear end and here you go bustin' on me. I was so freaked out. It was like; I gotta at least give some kind of warning before pullin' the trigger."

Jack started laughing. "You did great. I thought it was all over. When I was running toward the boat and saw you weren't there, I thought one of them had grabbed you. How did you end up back on the island anyway?"

Kai drew a deep breath as if trying to build the courage to relive the episode. "I saw they were workin' on surroundin' you and tryin' to cut you off at the water. You looked like you could beat two of 'em, but the other one had an angle. I couldn't do anything to help you from inside the boat, so I grabbed the flare gun and climbed off from the opposite side, so I wouldn't get spotted. When I got to shore, I was crawlin' in your direction and you started runnin' the wrong way, away from the water. Then when you tripped, that's when I jumped up. Man, I was shakin' so bad and everything seemed like it was spinnin'. When you yelled shoot, I just closed my eyes n' pulled the trigger. Believe me, it was dumb luck that I even hit the stinkin' thing."

"Your dumb luck saved my butt."

"Yeah, well don't make a big deal about it. We've got a long night ahead of us. You better call Pop back. He's gonna be itchin' to hear what's up."

Jack made the call, and told Pop the whole story while Kai moved to the bow and began guzzling down bottles of water, one after another. He was still shaky from the whole ordeal, and seemed to be in a daze as he stared blankly at nothing in particular.

Pop was more relieved than excited about their success. He knew deep down it had been a huge mistake to let the boys go back to the island by themselves. Once again, he cautioned Jack to keep moving through the night and to stay as far away from the river's edge as possible. He reminded Jack to be alert for the unexpected on the Matanzas River during the full moon. There was no way to be sure their escape was complete, and daylight was still nearly seven hours away.

Bad Latitude was making slow and steady progress up river at trolling speed. There was no need to go faster as they planned to stay on the river throughout the night. Strangely, there was virtually no other boat traffic on the Intracoastal. The cloud cover had lifted and the sky was dotted with millions of stars. They were approaching the Matanzas Bay, under the glow of the full moon, causing the surface of the water to sparkle with a silvery light. The Castillo loomed in the distance as they passed below the *Bridge of Lions*. Jack noticed that most of the slips at the municipal dock were filled and the harbor was crowded with moored sailboats. The cabin lights were off in nearly all of the vessels, adding to the sense of isolation.

"Hey Kai, you want to give me a hand? Let's put the cooler inside the boat so it'll be safe, just in case we have to go fast again. It would really suck, after all of this crap, to have a strap break and lose it overboard."

"I hear that," mumbled Kai as he stumbled toward the stern from his perch at the bow.

The cooler was safely stowed on the rear deck, and the boys relaxed, sitting at the helm eating sandwiches. Kai was working on his fifth bottle of water when his mouth flew open. The water gushed down his chin onto his chest as he elbowed Jack and pointed toward the inlet.

"Tell me I'm seein' things Rackham," was all he could manage.

Jack, expecting the jokes were about to begin again glanced casually in the direction where Kai was pointing. Opening and closing his eyes several times, not believing what he was seeing, his answer came in a choked voice. "Kai, I see something that looks like an old three masted ship. How about you?"

"That's what I'm seein' and there's some kind of green fog stuff all around it. Everything else is nice and clear. Whaddya think it is?"

"I know it's impossible, but it looks like an old pirate ship. It has a flag with the skull and crossed cutlasses, just like the Rackham flag, but there's nobody on deck."

"Great. It's a Rackham reunion out here on the briny deep. Figures you'd have a relative that was a cutthroat. He's probably gonna try to steal the treasure." He paused and shook his head. "Listen to me. I'm startin' to believe this stuff. It has to be our imagination. We're both just freaked out and got all that full moon crap goin' on in our heads. It's gotta be some kinda mirage," insisted Kai.

"How can both of us see it if it's a mirage? Hey look, it's changing direction and now that mirage is heading our way. This makes no sense. There's no wind and its sails are full. It's gotta be a ghost ship."

"Knock it off with the ghost stuff. It's gotta be our imagination," said Kai.

"Well, now our imagination is turning to port like it's trying to block our way up river."

"Blockin' our way nothin' it's aimin' cannons at us."

The words were barely out of Kai's mouth when a loud explosion rumbled from the ancient ship, followed by a puff of thick gray smoke. *Bad Latitude* was still moving at trolling speed at the sound of the blast. Seconds later, a geyser of water erupted from the river barely ten feet from their starboard beam. Jack shoved the throttle forward to gain speed and began a zigzag pattern in the direction of the ship.

Kai abandoned the mirage theory. "Ain't we headin' the wrong way Cap'n?"

"I'm open for suggestions. Fill out the card and put it in the glove box. I'll read it later."

"Very funny. I just had this idea that maybe goin' the other way might make more sense you dimwit."

"We don't have a choice. They can't get an accurate fix on us or lower the cannon enough to hit us if we head toward them at high speed. If we go the other way, a looping shot might just get lucky, besides, we don't know where our island buddies might be by now."

"Whatever. Might as well go out with a bang."

Bad Latitude planed out quickly and handled like the high tech machine that it was designed to be. As Jack predicted, the cannon shots were now well off the mark, sailing harmlessly over their heads. He kept the boat moving back and forth creating a rotating target from the ship's bow to stern to force the ship to attempt clumsy adjustments. Within a hundred yards of the ghost ship, Jack made a daring course change, making it appear that they would cross the bow of the ancient wooden vessel. At the last moment, he pulled the wheel hard to starboard cutting behind the ship's stern to within a few feet of the rudder. Now faced with the choice, he hugged the south side of the inlet and aimed his boat toward the open sea.

Jack turned to look back toward the harbor to check on the progress of the old frigate. It was as if time stood still and he felt a deep chill while heavy beads of sweat stung at his eyes. The ship was nowhere to be seen. Turning back toward the sea, the heavy green mist now stretched across the inlet blocking their exit. Not wanting to venture through the mysterious fog, Jack swung the boat hard to port and aimed toward the center of the harbor. Kai, remained speechless as the chase continued, holding onto the T-Top rail as Jack continued to push *Bad Latitude* to its limits.

In the distance came the crack of another cannonball being launched and Jack instinctively swerved to the opposite direction of the sound. Kai lost his hold and fell face first against the inside of the gunwale as they went into a sideways skid across the water's surface. Jack fought furiously to regain control as another shot rang out. This time, the ordinance nearly found its mark and the concussion lifted *Bad Latitude* from the surface for an instant, causing the propeller to screech as it left the water. As the boat slammed against its own wake, Jack was thrown forward into the wheel, knocking the breath out of him.

The cannon fire continued from the now invisible vessel and a newly formed heavy green mist was blocking the northern side of the harbor. The only logical option was to turn south in the direction of the giant cadavers that had chased them on the island a few hours earlier. It was their only chance. They had to hang on. First light was still three hours away.

21

Stalkers

Kai dragged himself from the deck. Blood was oozing from the two-day-old stitches below his eye. Wiping the leaking wound on his shirtsleeve, he looked south through the harbor toward the old bridge. The surface of the water below the span was beginning to take on the same yellow green haze that was blocking their other escape routes. *Bad Latitude* was running at full speed while Jack continued a sweeping serpentine evasion track through the small bay. Unable to yell above the engine noise, Kai began waving and pointing wildly to get Jack to look toward the bridge at the menace forming ahead. They were being pinned inside the harbor and, as the mists were closing in on them, the sound of cannon fire continued. Finally, Jack noticed the fog collecting underneath the bridge and slowed the engine trying to figure out what to do. The boys were less than three hundred yards from the municipal dock, which was thirty yards beyond the bridge and the strange fog below. There was no choice, they had to take the risk, get to the dock, and abandon the boat. Jack gunned the engine once again, just as the water heaved on their port side as another shot nearly found its mark.

As the fog thickened, *Bad Latitude* burst through the no wake zone below the bridge separating the green glow temporarily. Cutting the engine back just enough to veer inside the pier area, Jack banged the boat roughly into one of the few open slips. He hoped the damage would be minor. There would be no chance to check until daylight arrived, if they lasted that long.

There was only time to tie off the spring line at the gunwale. They dashed to the stern and collected the cooler. The mist was rapidly enveloping the dock and their skin crawled as they felt the sticky moisture overtaking them. Running awkwardly down the pier, Jack remembered he had left the cell phone on board. Returning to the boat to retrieve it was out of the question, which made calling for help virtually impossible. The pair would be on their own and on the move until daybreak, which was now more than two hours away.

As they breathlessly reached the sidewalk connecting the pier to the street, Kai dropped his end of the cooler and bent over with both hands on his knees. "We gotta lose the cooler. There's no way we can run into town with this crate between us."

Reluctantly, and with a quick look over his shoulder, Jack agreed and they broke the top loose and removed the three bags from inside.

"Whatever happens, we have to stick together. We just need to make it until dawn."

"Great, like *Dawn of the Dead*," complained Kai. "Let's get movin'. I hate to tell you, but somethin's walkin' toward us through that fog."

Jack didn't waste time turning to verify the news and the boys, struggling with the heavy bags, bolted across the roadway into the ancient city. It didn't take long to realize that the weight of the bags would prevent them from keeping up a fast pace for any length of time. They had to keep moving while conserving energy. It was going to turn into a deadly game of hide and seek with short bursts of movement from street to street and shadow to shadow. As Jack turned south onto Charlotte Street, Kai grabbed his arm nearly tackling him in the process.

"We can't go that way," Kai explained in a frantic whisper. "That direction leads to dead ends at the San Sebastian River. North into the city is our only choice."

Turning, they half ran half jogged for two blocks. Reaching the notorious Treasury Street, they paused to make sure it was empty before crossing. It wasn't. Fifteen feet from the intersection, two of the decomposed stench ridden guards were limping their way methodically, but quickly, up the narrow roadway in their direction. There was nothing to do but sprint past in full view of the walking corpses. As they crossed, they were greeted with the blood curdling screams of their pursuers. By now, their legs and arms ached from the exertion and their chests heaved as they filled their lungs with rasping gasps. The gold became heavier with each stride.

Kai took the lead and turned west onto Hypolita Street. Not looking to see if the guards were gaining ground, the boys turned north onto Cordova Street and ducked into the courtyard of one of the many restaurants. As they tried to compose themselves and catch their breath, the unmistakable odor of the oncoming warriors became overwhelming. There would be no time for rest. Daylight was still an hour away.

As Kai and Jack were busy running for their lives, Pop was struggling to make his hat selection for the day. After five full minutes, he decided to go with the same hat he had worn for the last four or five days. It didn't matter that it had the name of a surfboard maker on it. He hadn't surfed in years. He liked the logo and the color black matched most anything. Pop was in a particularly upbeat mood and couldn't wait to congratulate the boys on their success.

Jack had asked him to meet them at seven but Pop decided it would be a great start to the day watching the sunrise at the downtown harbor with an extra large cup of coffee in hand. Throughout the night, he had resisted many urges to call Jack to check on their progress. They had accomplished their task and didn't need a mother hen keeping track of them. Grabbing the keys to his bright red Ram 4 x 4 quad cab pick up truck, he practically skipped through the back door, smiling like the happy man that he was. The first signs of light were peeking toward him as he drove into town along the coastal road.

"There's still a third one out here somewhere," Jack whispered.

"It's like they know every move we're gonna make. I can't go much longer," Kai panted.

"Just a little bit more, it'll be daylight in fifteen or twenty minutes."

"So what happens at daylight? Do they just go *poof* and disappear back to the grave or what?" asked Kai as he readied himself for another sprint.

"I'm not sure what happens. I just assumed they couldn't be out during the day."

"You gotta be freakin' kiddin' me! I'm holdin' out 'til dawn, runnin' and tryin' to stay alive and *NOW* you're tellin' me you just *ASSUMED* everything would be okay once the sun came up?"

Kai didn't wait for an answer and took off in a semi crouch toward Tolomato Street. Daybreak was just around the corner and so was the third corpse, waiting, with outstretched hands at the intersection. There was no time for Kai to react as exhaustion had taken over and the weight of the gold threw him off balance. He tried to stop before running headlong into the rotted chaser but stumbled forward and fell, landing hard, head first, at the feet of the dead guard. The race was lost.

The walking cadaver reached Kai with his clammy disfigured hand and swept him up from the pavement by the hair. Kai was face to face with the loathsome creature and the other two were moving in, ready to join the slaughter. They were still regenerating. Internal organs were forming, and body fluids pulsed through openings not yet covered in skin, leaking stringy sticky pink trails. The pungent smell of decay filled the air.

The wind had been knocked out of Kai during the tumble and he was unable to make a sound. There was no sign of Jack and he closed his eyes, swallowing hard, waiting for the end.

In the next instant Kai found himself falling to the ground as the evil screams erupted again all around him. Scrambling to his knees, he could see the corpse lying on the road with a pipe shoved through a gushing eye socket. With new energy Kai jumped to his feet in time to see Jack run toward the other two Indian guards with a wooden trash can held high over his head. The can was thrown wildly, missing both, but caused them to separate for a moment. It was enough to give the boys the break they needed to escape. Kai grabbed the gold-filled bag as they ran down Tolomato Street, putting some distance between themselves and the dead warriors.

"Come on, jump the fence we can buy some time in here," yelled Jack.

"Are you nuts? This is the old cemetery. Whaddya tryin' to do, make it easier for 'em?"

"Don't argue. We can keep the gravestones between them and us, at least 'til daylight. We can't keep up this pace. Hurry, they're heading this way!"

Jack hopped the fence and reached back to give his friend a hand. It was then that Kai noticed that Jack wasn't carrying the other bags.

"Where's the loot?"

"Who cares about that now? Get your butt moving. We can hold out for ten more minutes."

"Oh yeah, your daylight theory. I gotta lot of confidence in that one," complained Kai in a huff as he crawled over the top of the rusted wrought iron fence.

Running and ducking behind the old headstones and crypts was their last remaining hope. They weren't surprised to see the guards separate to try to surround them as they had on the island. The third had recovered from being impaled and joined the chase with the pipe sticking through the back of its skull. Daylight was minutes away and the guards seemed to move with a new sense of urgency. There was no way that the boys could hold out for much longer. All energy was spent and their bodies were giving out. In a low crouch, they worked their way toward the street side fencing and hid themselves behind an ancient tomb. It must have been the resting place of someone very wealthy as it was the largest mausoleum in the cemetery. Finally, the sun broke clear above the horizon and Jack, too tired to continue, held his breath hoping his daybreak hunch had been right.

Pop was enjoying his coffee as he walked down the pier to scan the harbor. He figured the boys would probably stay out on the water a little longer, docking soon after dawn. His light-hearted mood changed to panic when he saw the broken cooler at the edge of the walkway. Walking faster, he made it two thirds of the way down the pier when he spotted *Bad Latitude*. Seeing the haphazard way it had been docked, he dropped the coffee and ran to his truck. His frantic search started directly across from the marina, with a systematic block-by-block drive through the city. His hands trembled and the second-guessing began all over again. Something had gone very badly. Mother hen or not, he should have stayed in touch with them throughout the night.

To Pop's great relief, he found the boys, collapsed in the shadow of the old mausoleum, the names, and dates having been worn away by the elements over three centuries. They appeared bruised and battered but otherwise fine. Exhaustion had caught up with them but sunrise had been their rescuer. Jack's theory had been right.

"Now that I see the two of you are okay, do you mind tellin' me why you're layin' here in an old graveyard? So much for stayin' out on the water away from the riverbank."

Jack and Kai described everything that happened, including the appearance of the ghost ship flying the Rackham flag and the details of the chase through town. Pop listened intently, his heart racing as he grasped just how close the two had come to not surviving the night.

"I wish you had taken the cell phone with you. I coulda been here in ten minutes."

"I know Pop. I remembered it too late and couldn't go back."

"Well, I'm proud of both of you. It took a lot of determination and guts," said Pop.

Kai picked himself up from the dirt and looked toward Jack. "Too bad we only got away with one bag of gold. We started out with three."

"Looks like that's gonna be worth plenty if you ask me." Pop patted Kai on the back as he continued. "What happened to the other two? Too much to handle during the chase, I suppose."

Kai began slowly, explaining the part that Jack had left out. "One of the dead creeps got hold of me and just when I thought it was over, Jack showed up outta nowhere and saved my rear end. He was helpin' me get away and I guess he left the other two bags in the street. Those old guard things probably took 'em back to the island when they disappeared."

Jack draped an arm around his friend's shoulder. "Don't worry about it Kai. I figure I owe you anyway. Do you think I'd let something happen to you over a little bit of gold?"

Kai held up the remaining bag. "Nah. Guess not. But it wasn't a little bit of gold. It was at least twice as much as this."

"It's okay. C'mon guys, let's get goin' before somebody thinks we're all nuts hangin' out in this decrepit old place. It's givin' me the creeps. We can grab some breakfast somewhere and then I can run this stuff to the safe deposit box," said Pop as he motioned for them to follow.

"Gimme a minute," hollered Jack as he hopped the old fence and dashed up the street to the corner. Kai and Pop looked at one another and shrugged, wondering what he was up to. A minute later, he was limping back to where they were waiting. He had both arms down at his sides, his lower half was blocked from view by the shrub-lined fence.

"Do you have more than one deposit box Pop?"

"I've got a big one and a little one. The big one should hold everything with no problem."

Jack started smiling again as he held up the two bags that Kai assumed had been lost. "You better get a couple more boxes Pop. These are gonna take up a bunch of space."

Kai flipped out. "*YOU* are a freakin' jerk. *YOU* let me babble on n' on like you were some great friend, the ultimate hero, lookin' out for me, and you knew you had the loot the whole time!"

Pop was ecstatic. He couldn't believe the weight of the three bags together.

After a huge bear hug for both boys, Pop ordered excitedly, "Let's get outta here, we gotta a lot to do, and you millionaires need to get some rest."

"Okay Pop. We've got one more job to handle before we go home." Jack reached into one of the bags and removed a few pieces of gold. Fumbling around inside another bag, he pulled out the skeletal hand of the old Indian King. He looked at Kai and grinned. "We won't be long. Besides, I gotta go get *Bad Latitude* taken care of. I was kinda in a hurry last night and did a pretty lousy job of docking it. I'll have to pay for the slip rental before they go n' tow it away. Can you spot me a twenty and drop us off at the marina?"

Pop laughed as he reached in his pocket. "Well, I guess I can trust you for twenty bucks. Now, for the last time, let's get outta here."

22

Kai's Revenge

Much to Jack's relief, there was only a minor scrape on the hull of *Bad Latitude*. He paid the dock master for the use of the slip and took a few minutes to clean up the mess they had left behind. After locking down the electronics, Jack stuffed the cell phone in his pocket and hurried down the pier to meet up with Kai, who had fallen asleep sitting on one of the benches.

"You gonna sleep all day or you gonna help me out with your big idea?"

Kai looked up at Jack with a pained expression. "Awwww geez. Can't we just chill out or somethin' for a little while?"

"Let's get this done Kai. We can hold out a little longer."

"You've been sayin' that all night. I'm beat."

With Kai lagging behind Jack walked across town to a wooded area nearly two miles from the marina. He stopped before reaching a dirt driveway guarded by a rusted mailbox sitting lopsided on a leaning wooden post. Within a few minutes, Kai caught up, complaining about sore feet and his desperate need of a shower.

Jack hunched down behind the hedgerow. "Keep your voice down. Is this it?"

"Yeah, this is the place. Kinda homey ain't it."

"Can we cut through the trees to make sure they're gone or are we stuck walking up the driveway?" whispered Jack

"Cut through the trees. You can see their place from this side."

They crept through the pines and brush as silently as possible, and eased their way to the side lot of an old ramshackle bungalow. The roof was rusted out tin and most of the windows were covered with plastic and duct tape. There was barely a trace of white paint left on the old wooden siding and the yard was littered with junk and piles of garbage. The stench was horrible. Inside one of the windows was an old fan covered in cobwebs, its blades rusted as badly as the tin roof. An old bathtub sat abandoned in the middle of the side yard. They needed to get to the front of the dilapidated house to see if the twins were home, requiring them to dash without cover across the yard. Kai suggested they wait to see if there was any noise from someone stirring inside. Jack agreed and they sat down in the row of scrub pines out of sight.

Twenty minutes turned into thirty and Jack was losing patience. "They must have left by now, it's almost nine o'clock. Let's give it a shot."

"That's easy for you to say. You're not the one that got his brains beat in by those idiots," argued Kai. "Can you even believe the way these guys live? I'm ready to puke smellin' that dump all the way over here. It's gonna get worse the closer we get. Do we hafta go inside?"

"It'll be worth it. Trust me. I'm going to make a run for it and see if their van is gone. I'll signal you from the corner of the house if the coast is clear."

"Yeah, sure, you got the daybreak thing right so you think you're on a roll now. They better be gone, that's all I'm sayin'."

Jack crawled from behind the pines to the edge of the cluttered yard before sprinting half stooped toward the corner of the house. One third of the way across the yard he heard the sound of the screen door slamming. He was caught in no man's land, too far from the house and too far from the safety of the woods. With the reflexes of a cat, he altered his course and dove behind the abandoned bathtub as the door slammed a second time.

"Why ain't we takin' the day off? We worked yesterday," grumbled one of the twins.

"If we don't pay those fines by Friday they revoke our bail and we git locked up, that's why stupid."

"Yeah, call me stupid. Yer the one that got the van stuck so's we'd go n' git caught n' hafta ....hey didjoo jus' see sumpthin' go scamperin' past in the yard over yonder?"

"Now yer seein' things ya idiot. No I didn't see nuthin', now git in the truck so we can git this job done n' paid fer b'fore we both end up the jailhouse."

Jack held his breath while Willie and Billy argued. Finally, both truck doors slammed. The van's engine cranked several times before finally sputtering to life, choking, and grinding while polluting the area with thick blue-gray exhaust. With the van's fan belt squealing at a deafening pitch, Willie and Billy finally bucked and coughed their way down the driveway and out of sight. Jack bolted for the corner of the house and pressed his back against the wooden siding where he waited; making sure it was safe, before motioning to Kai that all was clear. Joining Jack, Kai cautiously peered around the corner to confirm for himself.

"This can't be happenin'. I musta stepped in somethin'. Nobody's house could smell like this with people livin' in it," complained Kai while pulling his T-shirt up to cover his face.

Jack turned toward his friend with a straight face. "It's the security system."

"Security system? Whaddya talkin' about? Who in their right mind would wanna break into this dump? You couldn't rob this place without throwin' your guts up."

"That's what I mean. They keep it so gross; nobody would ever want to get near the place. That's their security system."

Kai wasn't amused. "Keep your wit to yourself. Let's get this over with before I puke on your shoes."

With one eye on the driveway, they walked up the two creaky steps onto the porch and past an abandoned washing machine.

"Well, we know they don't use that," muttered Kai.

The screen door had no screening. A sheet of plywood nailed onto rusted hinges was used as the front door and was left pushed back against the interior wall. Just inside the doorway was a concrete block. Jack assumed they used it to hold the plywood door closed at night since there was no latch or doorknob. The stench inside the house was worse than they had imagined and the boys gagged convulsively as they entered. Both had covered their faces with their dirty sweat soaked shirts, preferring to breathe the stale air from the previous night. They passed through the makeshift kitchen, filled with fast food take out containers crawling with maggots and roaches. It was all they could take as they settled on the easiest and most convenient hiding spots for the trap they were trying to set.

Reaching into his back pockets, Jack extracted the gold pieces and the amputated hand of the dead Indian King. He handed Kai the old bones and, using his foot to open a bottom cabinet, shoved one of the gold pieces under the sink. Kai moved to the bedroom where he tossed the ancient remains into the back corner of a closet. He ran out of the house as Jack placed the last gold piece under a broken down chair. Still covering his face, Jack burst through the screen door on the run, leaping from the porch into the yard. Kai was already in the driveway, several yards from the house with his face uncovered, coughing, and spitting as he stumbled toward the road. Neither spoke for several minutes while they tried to get control of their gag reflexes.

Finally, Kai turned toward Jack with a devilish grin on his face. "How 'bout we stop n' get some bacon n' nice runny eggs?"

That did it. Jack's stomach couldn't hold out. Kai laughed out loud and walked into the street, as Jack lost it on the side of the roadway. After a couple of minutes, pale and sweaty, he caught up with Kai, wiping at his mouth with his shirt.

"That was rotten. You knew I was skeeved and ready to puke."

"Yeah, I know. Guess we're even on that snake trick you pulled on me," laughed Kai.

Jack smiled and grudgingly admitted the score was even. He started feeling better as they approached the marina.

Kai finally broke the silence. "So why'd we put the gold pieces in their house? Don't you think the hand woulda been enough?"

"Who knows if it'll work at all? If the dead creeps come looking for the bones or the gold tonight, the trail will lead to your buddies Willie and Billy. Those Zombie things can't get in the safe deposit boxes at the bank and there won't be any trace of anything at your house or mine. They were probably only guarding the king's remains but I figured we should cover both possibilities, instead of taking a chance."

"Yeah, but you said somebody else planted the gold in that guy's grave. It never belonged to that Indian dude anyway."

"I know, but it was still in the grave buried with him. When you were running toward the boat last night, one of those guards went right toward the cooler like he was going to snatch it up. The loot's still gonna have the scent on it. A few pieces won't matter for us anyway."

Kai conceded the point. "Makes sense I guess. All I want now is a dozen showers, 'specially after bein' in that pigsty. Who knows, the dead dudes might show up at that place one night and the smell and filth will drive 'em back to their graves empty handed anyway."

They climbed aboard *Bad Latitude* and motored across the bay toward the shallow waters off Villano Beach. Jack piloted the boat as close to shore as possible and cut the engine. After a quick thumbs up, Kai dove overboard from the bow and swam the last fifteen yards to shore. He had a two-block walk to reach his house. Jack turned the boat south and raced down the Matanzas toward home. Exhaustion was replaced by excitement, and he looked forward to rehashing the adventure with Pop and Nan. It was almost noon when he slid into the boatlift.

He was disappointed to find his grandparents gone. After cleaning the boat, he took a long hot shower and changed into clean clothes. Grabbing the cordless phone and a very tall sweet tea, he went out to the lanai, making himself comfortable in a poolside lounge chair. He dialed Talia's number. She answered on the first ring.

He nearly yelled into the phone. "Hey Talia. We did it! We pulled it off!"

"Yeah, I know, Val called a little while ago. She says Kai is sooooo psyched but he's got more cuts and bruises than before. What the heck happened?"

He described everything in vivid detail. Talia was horrified to hear how close the boys had come to being caught on the island. She agreed to meet Jack, Kai, and Val at the municipal dock for a trip to celebrate at their favorite waterside restaurant. It would be her last summer ride on *Bad Latitude*. By the time Jack hung up the phone, he was fighting to keep his eyes open. Soon he dozed off into a deep sleep.

The sound of the Escalade pulling into the garage startled Jack from his nap. The phone was still in his hand. Checking his watch, he saw that it was nearly five o'clock. He had been asleep for almost four hours. Climbing out of the lounge chair, he was welcomed with aches and pains in virtually every part of his body, with his legs hurting the most. Limping toward the back door, he was met at the porch by Pop who greeted him with a very serious look. Jack wondered why Pop seemed so bummed out.

"What's the matter Pop?"

"Nothin', everything's fine. Nan and I were with Mr. Farrell and his friend over at the lighthouse all afternoon."

"How's he feeling now?"

"He's doin' good and asked the same about you and your friends. He says he enjoyed the visit with you kids, the ghost, not so much. I called him this mornin' 'cause he's got a buddy that's an expert on coins n' such and I wanted to get his opinion about the gold and gemstones you guys dug up. The guy that helped me out years ago moved out of the area. Jim Cunningham, that's Mr. Farrell's friend, was amazed when he saw what you and Kai brought back and spent hours taking pictures and making an inventory of everything so he could work up an accurate estimate of the value. He was very thorough and seemed to know his stuff."

"So does he think what we dug up is gonna be worth much?" pried Jack

"He said he'd like to get another opinion on the gems, and asked if it would be okay to get a friend of his to look at what you found. The other guy is a gemologist. I told him I would have to ask you and Kai, since you guys own it, but that I didn't see a problem. If it's okay with you guys, he said he could have him here in a couple of days," explained Pop as he sat down in one of the chairs.

Jack was just getting ready to repeat his question about the value when Nan walked out to meet them. She cut him off as he opened his mouth. "Did you tell him yet?"

"Tell him what?"

"He's got to be itching to hear what Mr. Cunningham said about the treasure. Don't tell me you've been going on and on, letting him squirm over this."

"Hey, there has to be a little drama. I wanted to see if I could get 'im to ask a few more times before I told him what the man said. Don't go ruinin' my fun."

"Oh you're awful. I can't believe you could do this after all he went through to get it. You're being cruel making him wait. If you don't tell him, I will," insisted Nan.

"Well, the way I see it, Kai should be here to hear this news at the same time. They're partners in this if you recall," answered Pop with a smirk.

Jack slapped his hand to his forehead and leaned back into the lounge chair when Nan agreed they should all wait for Kai.

"I don't think he would mind if you told me first. I'll call him right away. Hey, maybe we can call him now and just put the phone on speaker."

Nan wasn't changing her mind. "No Jack, now that I think about it, I agree with your grandfather. I think I'll call to see if Kai can come over." She turned abruptly and walked into the house.

Pop laughed out loud. "Glad I haven't lost my touch. I always did somethin' like this every Christmas to your dad and uncle. They'd get so annoyed. I'd make 'em wait around to open presents 'til I had my teeth brushed, hair combed, and a cup of coffee in my hand. Lookin' back, I think gettin' under their skin was my way of gettin' even for all of their shenanigans during the three hundred and sixty four days leadin' up to that mornin'.

"Pop, you guys are making me nuts."

The words were barely out of his mouth when a grinning Kai, accompanied by Nan, walked onto the porch. They had been playing along together as part of the prank.

Pop removed a small notepad from the pocket of his cargo shorts and fumbled for his glasses. He was stalling once again for effect, but trying to act serious. Finally, he was ready to share the big news. The boys fidgeted. Jack bounced his knees rhythmically while Kai chewed what was left of his nails. It was pure torture.

Nan, smiling sweetly, turned to Pop. "Honey, how would you like a nice fresh cup of coffee before you get started?"

23

Reluctant Rescuers

The girls were waiting at the dock. Talia had always admired Jack's tendency toward promptness while Val had grown accustomed to Kai being at least fifteen minutes late for nearly everything. They had been waiting for more than half an hour and, during that time; the guys had not answered any of Talia's many phone calls or text messages.

"He probably can't hear the phone over the boat motor. Don't worry about it, they'll be here soon," assured Val.

Talia pouted. "Next year, we'll all have our licenses so we can drive instead of having to go everywhere by boat."

"I think using the boat is pretty cool. Jack always has it all shined up and looking great. Besides, pulling up to a dock at a nice waterside restaurant for lunch or dinner isn't something you get to do every day."

"I didn't mean it the way it sounded. The boat is awesome, unless you get caught in a storm like we did the other day. You have to admit though, it's not so great having your hair blow all over the place before you get where you're going."

"Nobody's looking at our hair. Just watch when we pull up to the restaurant and everybody in the place starts staring at us kids climbing off a nice boat with no parents or adults along for the ride. Who do you know gets to do that?"

"You're right. I just wish they'd hurry up or at least text."

Kai and Jack were rushing up river in *Bad Latitude*, anxious to celebrate their good fortune with the girls. They were ten minutes away and the noise from the wind and engine was drowning out the sound of the ringing cell phone. Nan had helped them pick out some nice gifts and Pop had given them advances against the value of the treasure so they would have the cash they needed. The shopping spree had put them behind schedule but the guys knew that being late would be easily forgiven, especially once the girls saw their presents.

Earlier Pop had explained, after his game of suspense, that Mr. Cunningham's conservative estimate on the value of the treasure would end up bringing in around eighteen million dollars. It would net out somewhere between five and six million dollars for each of them, after taxes and related fees were deducted. The value could go even higher, depending on the results of a more detailed evaluation by the gemologist. There was the chance that the emeralds could be worth twice as much as he predicted, since most of them were huge.

All of the gold and gemstones had been safely stowed in four large safe deposit boxes earlier that afternoon. Nan was so excited; she arranged a summer ending party at the house for the next day. Pop warned Jack and Kai to keep the news of their find to themselves. They could tell only their parents, Val, and Talia for now. If word got out before the paperwork was completed, it would be nothing but aggravation.

Finally, the girls caught sight of Jack's boat veering toward the dock. The running lights were on, even though it wasn't yet dark, and Kai was waving excitedly from the bow. Talia and Val hurried up the gangway ready to board as soon as the boat pulled alongside the floating platform. The boat glided to little more than a pause at the municipal pier and within seconds, they were aboard and underway. Val hugged Kai as soon as her feet hit the deck. Talia and Jack waited long enough for the boat to move away from the pier.

They arrived at Cap's ten minutes later and Jack docked the boat with relative ease between two yachts. As Val had pointed out earlier, everyone's attention was riveted on them as they climbed from *Bad Latitude* onto the gangway. They were met by a hostess and shown to a waterside table where they wasted no time in placing their orders.

Over a dinner of several varieties of fresh oysters, the boys answered more questions about their adventure and their narrow escapes. They didn't share details of the estimated value of the treasure nor did they tell the story of their visit to Willie and Billy's house. They had just polished off their meal with the best key lime pie on the planet when Kai decided it was time to give the girls their gifts.

Kai, bandaged and bruised, tried awkwardly to begin the presentation before embarrassment took over. "Now that you know the story, we, uh, thought it, uh, would be nice to get you somethin' special." He motioned to Jack to jump in to help but Jack was too amused watching Kai bumble along to let him off the hook right away.

Kai was relieved when Jack finally came to his rescue. "What he's trying to say, not too well I might add, is that it's been an awesome summer, and we wanted both of you to have something nice to help remember it."

Val looked worried. "Is this like a going away thing?"

"You ain't gettin' rid of me that easy," interrupted Kai.

Jack was thrown off guard with Val's question. He didn't realize that his own attempt at explanation carried a final goodbye ring to it and wished they had paired off so they could have had some privacy. There was no way he was going to say anything remotely romantic, giving Kai something to pounce on to make a joke of later. Reaching into his pocket, with a nod toward Kai, he pulled out a small package wrapped in brightly colored foil. Following Jack's lead. Kai did the same, though the package was a different shape.

"What did you guys go and do?" Val's hands were shaking as she accepted her gift.

Kai reverted to his old self. "Awwww just open it will you. It ain't like they're engagement rings."

"It is jewelry though," Talia half stated, half asked.

"Guess you'll just hafta open 'em up to find out"

The girls were shocked when they opened the packages. Each contained identical diamond tennis bracelets arranged to surround a pair of beautiful diamond stud earrings. Val and Talia stared at the jewelry, then at the boys and then at each other. Val spoke up first.

"I love them, really I do, but this is too much. I can't accept something like this." Val was trying to be calm but her eyes were filled up and she left her seat to give Kai a hug.

"Val's right. They're beautiful and the thought is …. " Talia stopped for a moment before continuing. "I can't accept something like this either."

Jack and Kai looked at each other shaking their heads in unison. "How'd Nan know they were gonna do this?" questioned Kai testily.

"Who knows?" Jack barked as he turned to face Talia. "Listen, we just made a lot of money. It's not as big a deal as you're making it out to be. Nan already said she was calling Val's mom and your aunt to explain and said it would be okay. Nan even helped us pick the stuff out."

As if on cue, Jack's cell phone rang. It was Nan, and, following her orders, he put the call on speaker so that Val and Talia could hear. She explained that accepting the bracelets and earrings had been cleared already and they should go ahead and put them on without any more fuss. Nan went on to say that they needed to get back to the dock in St. Augustine within the next half hour. There was going to be a party tomorrow and Nan had received permission for the girls to spend the night. Val's mom would pick the girls up at the pier so they could run home and get clothes for the next day. Nan would pick them up at Val's house as soon as they were ready. The connection went dead as Nan hung up without waiting for a reply. Talia and Val kissed the boys and slipped into their new jewels. *Bad Latitude* was underway within a few minutes. Arriving at the pier, they found Val's mom already waiting. She was parked illegally with the motor running. The girls jumped from the boat and sprinted toward the car.

Two hours passed since they had dropped Val and Talia off at the dock and the boys were still hanging out on the deck above the boathouse, waiting for the girls to arrive. Now it was Kai's turn to be impatient. "What's takin' 'em so long?"

"How do I know? Guess they're getting even with us for making them wait earlier."

"You wanna play Madden?" asked Kai.

"If you want, but when they get here they're gonna want us to quit. What happens if, for once in your life, you're ready to beat me and they show up?"

"Yeah, that would be my luck."

Jack laughed. "Listen to you. You gotta be kidding me. You just became a millionaire less than twenty-four hours ago. I think that's pretty lucky if you ask me."

Kai started laughing. "Geez, I forgot about that."

"Pop said it'll take three or four months for us to get our money. That'll give you time to let it all sink in and figure out what to do with it."

Nan and the girls finally arrived twenty minutes later. They were giggling and laughing their way through the back door into the lanai. Pop absently checked his watch as if to somehow document their time of arrival and shook his head as he stood up from his favorite seat.

"I gotta get up early so I guess y'all can fill me in on what's so funny tomorrow," grumped Pop.

"No wait a minute. You have to hear this," said Nan as she walked over and grabbed him by the arm.

"How long's it gonna take?"

"Just sit tight a minute. You're not going to believe this story."

Pop sat down, clearly annoyed. "Don't you think there's been enough excitement for one day? I'm gettin' kinda tired of all these unbelievable stories."

Nan ignored him and turned to Val and Talia. "Tell them what we heard."

Val turned to Talia before she started. "We had to stop at the store to pick up a few things and bumped into Nina and Grant. They asked if we had heard the news about those smelly creeps, Willie and Billy."

Jack and Kai each sat forward in their seats. Pop tried to act disinterested. He never told Nan about how the boys had placed the bones and gold pieces in the twin's house.

Kai started making the *gimme* signal with his hands. "So what's the big story?"

"They found their van at the end of the driveway a couple of hours ago."

"Who is they?" asked Jack, now slightly nervous.

Val became indignant over the interruption. "The Sheriff's department."

"So what's the big deal about that? That probably happens twice a week." Kai started to get up but Pop grabbed him by the shirt.

"I'm trying to tell you guys the story if you would stop interrupting me." Val proceeded to explain that earlier, just after ten that night, a county deputy, on routine patrol, discovered Willie and Billy's van lying on its side in the driveway with the lights on and the engine running. The rear doors of the van had been ripped from the hinges and flung several yards from the vehicle in opposite directions. There were several strange footprints found surrounding the van, which all led to the wooded area at the side of their house. It appeared that something had been dragged into the woods. There were telltale signs of a struggle inside the house and a door that had been boarded up outside, had been broken wide open from the inside.

Kai almost blew it again with his mouth. "How could they see signs of a struggle in the middle of that dump?" Pop wished he had a roll of duct tape to wrap over Kai's yap.

Nan grew suspicious immediately. "How do you know it's a dump?"

Talia unwittingly came to Kai's rescue sharing her own observation. "Nan, they must live in a dump. You should see what these guys look and smell like. It's disgusting."

Kai breathed a sigh of relief, grateful for Talia's timely input.

Nan seemed content to let it drop and Val continued.

"Anyway, the Sheriff's Department is on a big time manhunt. They say foul play is suspected."

Jack and Kai were nervous. They had had a score to settle, but putting the Indian guards on the scent of Willie and Billy had been only a hopeful attempt at scaring the twins away, nothing more. This was sounding serious. Both squirmed as the story concluded. Pop made exaggerated eye contact with both boys, letting them know to keep their side of the story quiet. There was no sense getting everyone upset until more facts were known.

It was almost one in the morning when everyone decided to crash for the night. Pop had said his good nights half an hour earlier, reminding everyone that he had a very important appointment to keep first thing in the morning.

Walking through the gardens to the boathouse, Kai began panicking. "Whaddya think happened to 'em? Do you think they were taken to the island?"

"I don't know what to think. We have to ride over there with the spot lights and check things out."

"I ain't goin back there for anything or anybody," Kai shot back. "You're totally outta your mind."

"Yeah, well I'll go by myself then. I only wanted to scare them off to get even with them for beating the crap out of you. I didn't want them dragged off by the dead guys and end up dead themselves."

"You don't know for sure if that's what happened."

Jack changed direction and headed toward the boatlift, leaving Kai at the stairs to the boathouse loft. He was startled to find Pop waiting in the deck boat.

"Goin' somewhere?"

"Uh, …" Jack started to answer just as Kai came running up from behind. "Well, I guess I'm nabbed," he admitted.

"I knew you guys would be passing my way before too long. I'm goin' with you this time. We have to do what we can to make sure Kai's buddies don't reach that island," Pop ordered calmly. "C'mon, let's get after it."

"They ain't my buddies, but if the dead creeps grabbed the live creeps, I guess we gotta do somethin'. I can't believe I'm doin' this," groused Kai as he flopped onto one of the seats at the bow. The three headed off to Rattlesnake Island, and this time, gold was the last thing on anyone's mind.

Pop didn't take the usual care and precautions as the blue and white deck boat roared down the river at full speed. They all knew it was a race against time. If the twins were being taken to the burial grounds, the trio had to reach the island ahead of them. All three silently hoped they weren't too late. If the twins were already there, a successful rescue was unlikely.

"Pull the spotlights out and set them up. We should be there in a minute or two," Pop called out. "Figures the tide's goin' out already."

Kai reached under the bow seat and pulled out two spotlights along with a couple of flashlights. Pop slowed the boat as the red light on the depth finder blinked a warning that the water was getting dangerously shallow. Rather than anchor immediately, he held the boat in place with the throttle and gears as Jack and Kai began scanning the shoreline and island grasses for signs of the guards and twins. It was deathly quiet all around.

"I'll spin the boat so we can anchor up with bow facing the river for a quick getaway."

"There's no sign of anything. Maybe we should just hang here for awhile and use the spotlights to see if anything shakes out," suggested Kai, his voice quivering just a bit.

Pop was about to argue his case for going onto the island, when they heard splashing sounds headed their way through the water. Aiming the spotlights in the direction of sloshing water, the lights picked out the half drowned twins from the gloom. They were being dragged roughly between two of the rotting guards. Neither corpse was making any attempt at stealth as they waded machine-like toward the island.

Pop broke out in a cold sweat. Seeing the dead giants for himself brought a new perspective to the story of the chase from the night before. After the momentary lapse, Pop got it together but his worst fears were confirmed. If the twins reached the island, they would never survive the cruel treatment of the dead warriors.

"Kai, use the long gaff. Jack, grab that rope tied to the cushion. I'm gonna run right at 'em. See if you can take one of 'em out with the gaff hook Kai. Aim for its head. Gimme the boat pole just in case," shouted Pop in a determined tone. He turned his hat backwards as if getting ready for battle. "Jack, don't throw the lifeline 'til we take out the two…. whatever you call those nasty lookin' things."

With tools in hand and Kai holding onto the rail as best he could, Pop plunged the throttle all the way forward aiming the boat toward the corpse closest to the port side. In seconds, there was a loud thump as the hull smacked hard against one guard, barely missing the twins. At the moment of impact, Kai reached out with the gaff hook snaring the other monster at the neck. The skull flew into the air with a loud crack as it separated from the spine. The hold on the twins was lost and Pop spun the boat quickly to get in position to pluck the two thugs out of the water. Jack reached the pair with the life saving line and floating cushion on the first pass. He knew he had only one shot at it as one guard had already recovered from the initial impact.

The twin's eyes bulged in panic as they flailed for the rope. With only a moment to spare, they grabbed the line in time to be pulled from the reaching hand of the determined corpse. Pop dragged them along for several yards while Kai and Jack furiously reeled in the lifeline. It took every ounce of strength they had, and they just barely managed to pull Willie, and Billy over the side before breathlessly collapsing onto the deck.

Pop raced up river to the municipal dock. He offloaded the still shaking pair onto the boardwalk with a stern warning, poking each of them roughly with his fingers to their chests. "Don't even ask how we knew about this, but you'd better listen up. You guys gotta get as far outta town as possible, and I mean right now, or y'all will end up buried on that island. Trust me. It ain't over. Those dead things are probably shufflin' this way right now startin' their chase all over again."

He must have made the warning clear enough because Willie and Billie sprinted down the pier into the old town in a complete state of terror. Not even a wave or thank you was offered and neither turned to take a second look.

Positioning the boat away from the pier, Pop wiped the sweat from his forehead before looking toward Jack and Kai. "Guess now I'll have to explain our little midnight run to the missus. Whaddya say guys? Think we can go home and get some rest now?"

24

Wheels

Nan banged on the door to the boathouse to wake the boys for brunch. Twenty minutes later, they finally stumbled out, with all of their aches and pains, and found their seats at one of the poolside tables. Both were exhausted. Pop strolled into the lanai looking fresh and well rested, though he never actually bothered to go to bed the night before. He had a smug look on his face as he squeezed Jack hard at the top of his sore shoulder making his grandson wince.

"Can't hang huh?"

While Pop was busy teasing the boys, Kai's parents walked through the double doors, followed by Val, Talia, and Nan.

"Mark, Liz, it's been a long time. It's nice to see you folks again," greeted Pop warmly. "Y'all must be real proud of your boy here. He's a great kid."

After exchanging pleasantries, everyone took their seats at the tables. Nan had set up a buffet for the brunch. It was loaded with everything anyone could want and everyone dug in hungrily. As the meal was finishing Pop excused himself from the table and exited through the side door in the direction of the garage. No one thought much of it at first as everyone was busy talking about the late night rescue of Willie and Billy.

Fifteen minutes passed when Kai asked about Pop's whereabouts. Nan shrugged trying to suppress a smile, which only triggered Jack's curiosity. "Nan, seriously, where did Pop go? He's gotta be up to something."

"He's probably hiding out, smoking one of his cigars. Relax; he'll be back soon enough."

Jack wasn't buying it. He knew Pop never smoked cigars in the morning, so he settled back to wait, knowing Pop probably had something outrageous up his sleeve. Within a few minutes, there was a ruckus coming from inside the house followed by a pair of familiar voices.

"Are we too late for breakfast?" came the voice of Jack's dad.

"I like my eggs over easy," Uncle Chris hollered.

Jack jumped from his seat and rushed to the back door. "What are you guys doing here?"

Pop was bringing up the rear following his two sons into the lanai from the house. "I thought maybe these two chuckleheads would like to join today's little party."

Jack tried to get to his dad and uncle but was cut off by Nan. She hugged both of her boys tightly at the same time.

"See Mike, I told you I was her favorite. Mom hugged me first," teased Uncle Chris.

"Yeah right. Mom wasn't trying to hug you. She was putting her arm up to push you away."

Nan assured them individually that each was her favorite and laughed at the ruckus they were making. Pop stood back chuckling at the antics while Talia and Val giggled at the way the family constantly teased one another.

Finally, Jack's dad hugged his son. "I hear you guys found some loose change lying around. Congratulations."

"Yeah, right, loose change. It was little more than that Dad," laughed Jack. "Where's Mom and Belle?"

"They couldn't make it this trip. We're leaving when you leave."

"You guys flew all the way down here for one day?"

"That was the plan, but we heard there's a hurricane moving this way so maybe we can stretch it out. Pop's going to need a hand getting everything battened down and it's been a long time since I saw a hurricane up close. I didn't think you would mind trading a couple of school days for some decent waves."

"Cool. The surf will be churned up big time the day before it hits," said Jack.

Uncle Chris was pouring a cup of coffee as Nan moved next to him. "So have you met a nice girl yet Christopher?"

He hated being called Christopher and dreaded questions about his continued bachelor status. "Mom, I have plenty of time. I'm holding out for perfection."

Nan rolled her eyes. "Well, while you're holding out, your hair isn't. You're starting to get gray hairs in your beard. You'd better start using some of that hair coloring for men or the ladies will start to think you're an old goat." Shaking her head she moved back to the table while Jack's dad grinned, catching his brother's attention by rubbing his chin as if it itched.

Uncle Chris wasted no time firing back at his brother, "At least I can grow one."

Pop moved between the tables and waited for everyone to settle back into their seats.

"Geez, I hope we're not getting a lecture," barked Mike.

Uncle Chris laughed. "Well, if we are, it's probably about something that you did."

Not waiting for the conversations to stop Pop plowed on with his congratulations. He made it a point to commend the boys on their determination and willingness to persevere when things seemed stacked against them and for looking out for each other. Finally, he wrapped everything up. "You guys showed a lot of character going back to that island to rescue those guys that beat up Kai. I'm proud that both of you were able to look past that. There's no doubt that the two of you saved their lives. Y'all just bein' good-hearted young fellas makes me prouder than anything else. Well, that's enough jawin'. Would everyone please follow me to the garage? We have a little surprise for these guys."

Without further pause, Pop walked out through the screen door. He was waiting by the garage with the door remote in his hand as everyone assembled. Once everyone was accounted for, Pop hit the button and the massive door rolled upward as he proudly announced to Jack and Kai, "You boys earned these".

The boys were stunned as they watched the door rise. Inside the spotless garage was a pair of brand new Jeep Wranglers, one yellow, one red. They were completely decked out with custom striping, off road tires on bright chrome wheels, lift kits, step rails, and customized chrome accessories. The interiors had been finely detailed with upgraded seats, sound systems, and padded roll bars. Key rings, one with Kai's initials in yellow, and one with Jack's in red hung from the mirrors. Pop hoped he had made the right color choices.

"Pop! They're awesome! You didn't have to go and buy these!"

"I didn't. You two bought 'em. I just loaned y'all the money 'til you get your salvage checks."

Kai clambered inside the yellow Jeep with Val at his side. "This is incredible," he repeated over and over again.

Talia climbed into the red one to join Jack. "I guess this is why your dad flew down."

"Whaddya mean?"

"You won't have your license for another month. Your dad's here to drive it home for you. This is so cool. I've never ridden in one of these."

"Hey Dad, are we driving this home?"

"That's the plan. Pop set this up a few weeks ago. We'll leave after the big storm passes."

Jack gave his dad the thumbs up and stared over at his grandfather. "When did you get these?"

Pop laughed. "I ordered 'em the day after you guys started diggin'. My buddy Matt Tatham did the customizing. He just finished the work late yesterday. When we all went runnin' after Willie n' Billy, it kinda messed up my plan. I was gonna get 'em last night, but since we had to go on our rescue cruise, your dad and uncle had to pick 'em up for me this morning. At least the surprise wasn't ruined."

"What would have happened if we didn't get the treasure?"

"Never crossed my mind. I knew you'd both come through."

Kai looked over at his beaming parents. "You guys knew about this too?"

"Since late yesterday," came the reply.

The boys raced off for test rides with their dads and the girls, traveling A1A to the State park and south down the beaches all the way to the inlet. They were gone for over an hour. In the meantime, everyone turned their attention to getting things in shape for one last summer bash.

Nan decided to save herself some work and had the event catered by the crew from The South Beach Grill. Everything was set up with a Caribbean theme. The sounds of Jimmy Buffet and Bob Marley filled the air as flickering tiki torches helped to light the huge lanai and surrounding walkways. Everyone that was invited attended. Pop and Nan's reputation for throwing great parties was unequaled. Mr. Farrell arrived partway through as did the man and wife that had been so kind to Jack and Talia when they had tied up to their dock during the storm. The caterers had to keep sending for more food from the restaurant to keep up with the crowd. Pop was heard to mumble, "It looks like no one ate a thing for the week leading up to this shindig."

Talia had to leave for her red-eye flight home. It had cost Pop two hundred and twelve dollars to change her ticket so she could stay for the party and she left at the last possible minute. She and Jack managed to sneak away for a little privacy and made plans for him to visit at her new home. He would get the chance to meet her family within a few short weeks.

Jack returned to the lanai once Talia was on her way. Pop had abandoned the party and Jack found him in the study standing in front of one of the large bookcases. He was staring at an enlarged photo of a very tall man, wearing a suit and tie, holding a little baby in the palm of one very large outstretched hand. Standing next to the man, looking up at the baby, was a well-dressed lady much shorter than the man. The baby was smiling, showing no sense of fear while balancing more than six feet above the ground. Jack had never noticed the photograph before.

After a thoughtful pause, Jack walked in through the double doors. "Whaddya doing Pop?"

"Oh I needed to get away from all the hubbub for a bit and thought maybe I'd do a little work on my next project," came Pop's reply as he put the picture back in its place.

"Who's that in the picture you're looking at?" asked Jack.

"That's a picture of me when I was much younger."

"It sorta looks like you, but you're not that tall. The lady's definitely not Nan. Nan's almost as tall as you."

"You can't recognize me after all the time we've spent together? I should feel insulted."

"Seriously, who is it?"

Pop chuckled. "The little lady in the picture is my mom and the tall man next to her, holding the baby, is my dad..."

"And you're the baby being held up in the air." Jack finished.

"You've got it kid. I guess it was the eyes that gave it away."

"Yeah right. The picture's in black and white so how could I tell by the eyes. How old is that picture anyway?"

"It was taken when I was about eight months old. My parents were in their mid twenties. You can do the math, but I'm not admittin' to anything past thirty nine."

"Wow! Now that I look at it closer, you look a lot like both of them."

"Yeah, I guess I do," answered Pop with a heavy sigh. "You're lookin' at the best parents a kid ever had."

Sensing that Pop was getting emotional, Jack quickly changed the subject. He noticed the computer screen was lit up with a word document. "So whaddya working on?"

"I'm just fiddlin' around with a new story and took a little break," Pop replied absently as he walked to his big leather chair and sat down. The lack of sleep was starting to show. There was a dark puffiness showing below Pop's blue bloodshot eyes.

"So what's this book going to be about?"

Pop carefully propped his feet on the desk corner. "Oh, it's been underway for about six weeks now. I'll probably have the first draft done in a few days."

"How do you find time to write with everything else that goes on around here? You're always busy doing something."

"It's no big deal. If it's somethin' you like, it never feels like work. Actually, it's relaxing and the pages usually fly. My grandfather was the master storyteller. He could keep me spellbound for hours with his tall tales when I was growin' up."

"He's the one that gave you all those old books."

Pop nodded and smiled.

"So, getting back to the first question, what's this one about?"

Taking his feet down from the desk, Pop straightened a few papers that seemed out of order, trying to stall. Knowing he had no choice but to answer the question he let out another tired sigh before replying. "For the short version, the story's about the local St. Augustine area, a group of young kids, beach parties, fishin' trips, a haunted lighthouse, a ghost ship, dead Indian guards, a couple of bad guys and a successful treasure hunt. Sound familiar?"

"You're writing about me n' Kai?"

"Is that okay with you?"

"Whaddya kidding me? It sounds awesome. Are you going to use our real names?"

Pop thought about that for a second. "Yeah, I think so. By the way, I asked Kai's mom about his name when I started scratchin' out the storyline. Do you know what it means?"

"He told me a long time ago but I don't remember. What's it mean, little guy with a big mouth?"

Pop laughed at that one. "It means Gift From The Sea."

"Some gift. Lucky they didn't throw him back."

"Awww c'mon. He's a good kid."

"Yeah, I know. So what are those charts spread out on the drawing table? Got something new in the works? Another treasure hunt maybe?"

"Nothin' much gets past you, does it kid? As a matter of fact, I've been followin' several leads about stockpiles of gold that belonged to a really nasty pirate, our ancestor, good old Jack Rackham, otherwise known as Calico Jack. I believe you may have run across him recently. He was mean and ruthless, and left stashes of gold behind that were never recovered. There are clues of a treasure on a tiny island just east of Jamaica, as well as a cache tucked away in the Bahamas. In my travels, I managed to get my hands on an engraved copper plate that his wife, Anne Bonny, had in her possession up until the time of her death. It describes, in coded clues, all of the locations of Rackham's gold. It will take some more study, but I'm all over it and I'll get it sorted out soon enough. I was thinkin' maybe you, me n' Kai might be lookin' for somethin' to do next summer. You wanna try your luck again?"

"This is incredible Pop. Sounds like next summer could top this one."

"Probably. This one was just a practice run gettin' ready for next year. Oh, I meant to tell you. I want you guys to get your diving certificates. Next year, we're goin' to the islands and we're gonna be doin' some underwater work."

"Will we fly over there and rent a boat?"

Pop smiled. "Funny you should ask. I've been holdin' out on you again. Actually, I bought another boat. It's being fitted out now and should be ready in four or five months. She's a two masted schooner and I'm having bigger engines added, along with all new electronics and radar. The builder is also changing out all of the rigging, and renovating every square inch of her, inside and out."

Jack was laughing and shaking his head. "You're full of surprises. I hope Nan knows about *this* one. Sounds like it cost a few bucks more than that fancy old Chris-Craft. You won't get off the hook by naming another one after her."

"Nan knows all about it. She went with me to make the deal. This one's called *Reckless Endeavor*, an eighty-two footer, and she's a real beauty."

"Eighty-two feet? That's huge! It's kind of an odd name for a boat, especially since it sounds like wreck. Maybe you should change the name."

"Can't Jackman. I'm not too superstitious myself, but I've always been told that it's bad luck to change the name of a boat once she's been launched. No need to test that tale to see if it's true. Don't worry, she's very solid and seaworthy and, when I her get done, she'll be even better. Oh, almost forgot, the builder is flying down here next week to check out *Bad Latitude*."

"For what?"

"He's making a detailed pattern of your hull to use for designing a cradle and davit system on the stern of *Reckless Endeavor* so we can take your boat with us and hoist it in and out of the water. *Laffin' Gaff* is too big to haul and *Reckless Endeavor* draws several feet of water so we'll use yours to get back and forth to shore. I ain't kayakin' to some island or anywhere else for that matter."

"Do you have any pictures of it?"

"Yeah, but I want you to see her in person when she's ready to sail. Right now, she's under construction and not exactly looking her best. Now stop your pryin'." Pop paused to open the top drawer of his desk. "Speaking of pictures, that reminds me. Mr. Farrell gave me your camera. He said you must have dropped it during your visit."

Jack felt a shiver as he remembered the continuous flash of the camera during his encounter with the ghosts at the lighthouse. Now was not the time to download. He had a pretty good idea about what he would find on the memory card.

25

The Shark Before The Storm

The day had started with such promise and should have put an exclamation point on the summer that only dreams are made of. Hurricane Frances had been upgraded to a category three and was due to make landfall near Daytona Beach within thirty-six hours. The waves crashing against the shoreline were six times their normal size and the water was crowded with surfers looking for the rare thrill of a big ride.

Jack and Kai were in the middle of the group. Both were aggressive surfers, risk takers some would say, bordering on rude at times. Needing a rest from the non-stop pounding, the boys paddled through the assembly of hopeful wave riders and sat cross-legged on their boards, floating just beyond the rolling swells that curled into what Kai called *surfboard motors*.

Kai was feeling bummed. "I can't believe summer's over."

"Hey, ten weeks of your crap is all I can stand. I've got to get out of here so I can get my life back together and at least pretend to be normal. After this summer, I'm gonna need a shrink." Jack took on a dubious look. "What happened to your arm?"

"Whaddya talkin' about?" Kai twisted his elbow straining to see. "Hmmm, guess I scraped it on the bottom or got nailed by somebody's fin." It was a small gash just below the point of the elbow where it wasn't very fleshy. The blood flowed freely, appearing worse than it felt as it mixed with the salt water.

"We better ride back and get it patched up at the first aid station. You're going to be inviting *Jaws* for lunch if you keep bleeding like that."

"It's just a scratch. Stop worryin'. Sharks go out to deep water when storms are comin'. Besides, there's never been a shark attack anywhere near here."

Jack wasn't to be put off. "How about that kid fishing last year near Ormond Beach? He got his rear end chomped standing in three feet of water."

"That was four years ago and the idiot went n' stuffed bait in his back pocket. He was practically chummin'. That doesn't count."

Jack started toward shore. "Well, you go on sitting here looking like a happy meal, I'm not hanging out to be the after dinner mint."

With the sigh of someone giving up on an argument too easily, Kai flopped onto his belly, and started kicking toward the distant beach, moving alongside Jack within a few seconds. He caught a movement to his right from the corner of his eye as they approached the line of drifting surfers ahead. "Check it out. There's a dolphin swimmin' our way."

Jack's eyes widened. "Dolphins travel in pods, or at least pairs, you moron. That's a shark sniffing out an entrée. Looks like you might be on today's menu."

Without waiting for a reply, Jack knelt on his board, cupped his hands around his mouth, and yelled out a warning to the group of surfers clustered on the seaside of the breakers ahead. Everyone turned and stroked wildly toward the safety of shore. Satisfied that the message was out, he resumed paddling with new vigor.

Kai paused long enough to keep the pair together, now accepting the fact that the circling shark had zeroed in on him. The fifteen yards to the curling white water looked more like a mile.

The bump came at the backside of a swell, before the wave crested. Kai twisted in the air, arms flailing, in a vain attempt to grab for whatever safety the surfboard might provide. Plunging below the surface, he realized that the sliver of fiberglass had become an anchor and he ripped desperately at the Velcro strap around his ankle trying to break free. At the precise moment the binding was loose, he launched himself, kicking off the bottom toward the foaming surf.

Jack spun at the sound of the erratic splashing and, straddling his board, frantically searched the rolling swells looking for his friend. He could see Kai's bright yellow Ocean Arrow long board bobbing rider-less as the shark's dorsal fin cut through the surface on a heading from right to left. Gripped by fear, he calculated his odds and options. Leaving Kai behind, with no attempt at rescue, never entered his mind. Jack abandoned the safety of his own board just as Kai rocketed from below the surface six feet away. The determined predator passed within two feet of Jack; homing in on the thrashing Kai, now struggling mightily to avoid the shark's already bared teeth.

It wasn't fair. Kai knew he was going to die, only a couple of months short of turning sixteen. It was a sad and terrifying reality. Staring into the gaping jaws of the lunging shark a yard away, he threw his hands out defensively, trying to postpone his painful death. It was a lousy way for a day of awesome waves, not to mention the perfect summer, to come to an end. He should have listened to Jack.

The initial pain came from the missile-like thud to the chest, causing the air to escape the lungs in one great heave, followed by an excruciating burning sensation from the upper thigh. Blood filled the surrounding water as a final jolt hammered Kai between the eyes, causing his bleeding, oxygen starved body to shut down. Swirling into unconsciousness, lungs filling with seawater, his body sank rapidly beneath the waves.

As Kai's shoulders touched down gently against the velvety sea bottom, the pain subsided and his unblinking eyes stared upward toward the surface. The rolling motion of the sea clutched at the sunlight, collecting a wondrous mix of colors, creating brilliant prisms. The mental video whirred along in slow motion, his summer adventures in the haunted ancient city replayed in his mind with unnatural clarity until his struggle to survive finally gave way to peaceful surrender.

26

Dr. Butcher

The first thing Kai noticed was the searing pain in his right thigh followed by a rhythmic pulsing inside his head. With great effort, he squinted against the bright lights, looking curiously at his strange surroundings. The blur began to fade and images became clear. There was a curtain track directly above and a bottle to the left with a clear tube leading to his arm. Carefully turning his head from side to side, a familiar face came into view and a muffled voice could be heard as the face inched closer.

"It's about time you woke up."

"Where am I?"

"On a beach in Bermuda."

"Huh?"

"You're in a hospital numb nut. Second time in less than two weeks. Where'd you think you were?"

"Why am I in a hospital? What's goin' on?"

Jack stared over at his friend. "Whaddya got amnesia or something?"

"Stop messin' around. What am I doin' here and why do I have this I V in my arm?"

Jack pulled a chair next to the bed but remained standing. "I better go get your family and let them know you're awake. They've been waiting for you to get out of la la land for two days."

Kai pulled himself up to a sitting position. He felt light headed and wished the drummer in his brain would take a break. "First tell me what's happenin' and explain why I'm here."

"You really don't know, do you?"

"Well, if I knew, I wouldn't be askin' now would I."

Jack flopped into the chair. "Do you remember anything?"

"I remember feelin' like I couldn't breathe and then I was like watchin' a movie and everybody around was yellin' and pushin'."

"You don't remember the shark?"

Kai took on a blank stare. He was trying to grab onto any shred of memory that might have been filed away. Finally, after a seemingly endless pause, he looked toward Jack and answered simply, "No."

Jack took a deep breath. "Maybe you should let me get everybody together and then we can all explain it. They went down to the cafeteria a few minutes ago. It won't take me long to chase them down."

"Just tell me what happened. How many times I gotta ask? Geez, my head is killin' me."

"Well, that's part of it. The doc said you would have an awful bad headache for a week or more once you woke up. That's kinda my fault I guess."

Kai was restless and impatient, giving Jack the *come on* gesture with both hands, making it clear that he wanted to hear the story without delay.

Without further prodding, Jack plowed ahead. "We were surfin' off Talbot Island. The waves were big because a hurricane was on the way. You cut your arm on something and were bleeding into the water. Of course, I told you to get to shore before some shark smelled it but, as usual, you wouldn't listen."

Kai groaned as he repositioned his legs. "Get to the point. You can bust on me later."

"Anyway, this big old bull shark attacked you, knocked you right off the board. You were trying to make it to the surf but it hit you like a torpedo with its jaws snapping. It's a wonder it didn't kill you on that first swipe. Once you were in the water, away from the board, you were toast. The shark hit you in the chest, and then tried to clamp down on your leg, but I shoved the end of my board in its mouth so only the bottom teeth got you."

Kai was wide-awake now and reached down to feel the tightly wrapped thigh of his right leg. "So it didn't get to actually bite me, only scraped my leg."

"Hey, if you want to call one hundred and sixty three stitches a scrape, that's fine by me. The problem was, after I shoved the board in its mouth, he thrashed, and the surfboard rammed you right in the head, knocking you out cold. I guess the shark decided you weren't tasty enough because once it shook the board, it took off for open water. Your lungs filled up with seawater and you sunk below the surface. We were in about ten feet of water and I kept diving to the bottom trying to find you before the current caught you and carried you off for good. It seemed like you were underwater forever. Luckily, I ended up stepping on you and reached down and grabbed your arm. I couldn't swim while I was dragging you so I just kept jumping up and down toward the beach trying to breathe and get help."

"In other words, I was drowning."

Jack shook his head. "No, actually, you drowned. A bunch of guys saw me struggling and came out to help and they carried you onto the beach. One of the guys told everybody to back away so he could take care of you. You're really lucky because he was a doctor. His name was Dr. Butcher. The guy is awesome and he's been keeping an eye on you ever since."

"You expect me to believe the guy's a doctor named *Butcher*? And whaddya mean he's awesome? What'd he have to do?"

"That's really his name. He's the one that did CPR on you and got the leg wrapped to slow the bleeding before the chopper got there to haul you here."

"They used a helicopter?"

"Yeah, a medivac unit from Jacksonville. You were in bad shape amigo. Doc Butcher has been here on and off since it happened. He wanted to keep you knocked out for a couple days because he was worried about some kind of brain swelling. I told him not to worry; you were used to having a swelled head."

"Very funny. So you're telling me I've been in some kind of coma?"

"Sort of like a coma, but on purpose."

After a brief silence, Kai spoke up. "You and this guy Dr. Butcher saved my life."

"Well, I might have helped keep the shark from biting you worse than it did, but it was Dr. Butcher that saved your life. I'm not sure I should be telling you this, but you were what's called clinically dead for about five or ten minutes. Nobody was sure you were even going to make it until about twelve hours passed. Your butt was in the ER and then ICU. You got moved in here a few hours ago when they said you'd be waking up soon."

"You know, I still can't remember the shark attackin' me but I kinda remember this weird sensation like I was lookin' down over a bunch of people that were crowdin' around somethin' on the beach. I can even picture you runnin' toward some truck or van."

"I was trying to collect blankets to wrap you in. You were in shock and the Doc wanted to get you covered up. At first, when he told me to get a blanket, I freaked because I thought you were dead and he needed to hide your face, like you see in the movies."

"This whole thing is bizarre. I wonder why I can picture you but can't remember the shark. Geez, my family must have been freakin' out big time."

"Yeah, you could say that."

Kai was trying to get his memory together. Confusion was written all over his face and nothing was registering. "I guess I slept through the hurricane."

"You didn't miss much. By the time it hit the coast, it was down to a tropical storm and nothing much happened. We had some short power outages and some trees fell down here and there, but mostly, it just caused a bunch of aggravation for everybody."

As Jack finished, Dr. Butcher walked into the room. He was nothing like Kai had pictured. Instead of the older gray haired type Kai assumed him to be, he was young with dark hair, and an almost black goatee, which he kept rather short. The eyes were a dark brown and he wore a sparkling white lab coat with his name stitched across the top pocket. A bright smile preceded the greeting as he extended his hand for introduction.

"Hello Kai. You're my newest favorite patient. I'm John Butcher, if my friend Jack here hasn't already mentioned it." The handshake was firm and the smile infectious.

"Jack told me you were on the beach when all of this happened and that I wouldn't be alive if it weren't for you," said Kai.

"Let's just say you were in some big trouble. Jacksonville Fire and Rescue's finest did an unbelievable job getting you here in a hurry. There was only so much I could do for you on that beach. I'm glad to see you're recovering well and there doesn't seem to be any trace of permanent damage. You'll be sore for a while and you'll need lots of rest. I can't release you to go to school for at least two weeks. I want that leg to heal with no chance for infection." Dr. Butcher continued, "You ended up with a pretty bad concussion and you'll be at least a week or more suffering with headaches and nausea. I'll stop back tomorrow and we'll see about getting you up and walking around." Dr. Butcher laughed. "I'll make sure you get one of those gowns that snaps closed in the back."

"How come I can't remember all the stuff that happened?"

Dr. Butcher was thoughtful for a moment before answering. "It was a very traumatic experience. You're brain probably blocked some of it out as part of a defense mechanism. The memory of the attack may return, maybe it won't. It's not a memory that I would want." He smiled once again and moved toward the door.

"Before you go, Jack told me you wanted me to stay asleep, so I've been knocked out for a couple days. Is that why I've been havin' all kinds of crazy dreams n' stuff?"

"That's part of it. We kept monitoring your brain waves up until late yesterday. It was a good sign that there was so much activity going on because it helped us to gauge the dosages of all the meds we were pumping into you. Now get some rest and we'll talk it all through some more tomorrow, before we kick your butt out of here. You're out of the woods and should be able to leave in a day or two. Dr. Butcher didn't wait for more questions and hurried through the door to the corridor.

Jack was the first to break the silence. "I'd better go get everybody up here. It's pretty wild that you can't remember the day at the beach but remember dreaming while you were knocked out. Must have been some crazy stuff. I never remember my dreams."

Kai pushed his way back down into a prone position and lowered the bed with the controller. "I'm feelin' so weirded out. Everything seemed so real, it's like, all locked in like everything really happened, but I know it's all just a nightmare or somethin'."

Jack's curiosity took over and he sat down once again. Kai's family would have to wait a little longer. "Sounds like a *Wizard of Oz* moment to me. Can you remember details and stuff or is it a bunch of strange crap all jumbled together?"

"It's all detailed. I can picture everything like it really happened. Some of it's probably just memories from the summer, you know, like hangin' out with you n' Val n' Talia, fishin' with Pop, surfin', the stuff we do every summer."

"Okay, so what's the big deal? Were you on a yellow brick road with a little black dog…?"

"Knock it off. You're jokes still suck. *That much* I remember. It's just a bunch of stuff that's freakin' me out and I can't believe how real it seems."

Jack finally understood that Kai was being completely serious, not that it happened very often. "What kind of stuff are you remembering?"

Kai turned his head slowly, his temples pulsing with pain. "You think I'm gonna tell you so you can start on me with your *Wizard of Oz* crap again?"

"No really, I'm sorry, you're right, it isn't funny. I just want to know what you were dreaming about. Who knows? Maybe some of it's true."

"Nah. This is some really extreme stuff, like ghosts in the lighthouse, some creepy yellow fog, and you n' me runnin' around in the dark gettin' chased by these corpse things."

Jack's mouth hung open. He was completely fascinated. "This stuff sounds awesome. It's like Stephen King comes to St. Augustine."

"The coolest part of the dream is about us findin' this box of buried gold and gemstones and the two of us becomin' millionaires. It gets repeated over n' over."

Jack couldn't stay in the chair anymore and moved to the foot of Kai's hospital bed. "Now you're starting to freak me out. Did you happen to dream about us getting our own brand new Jeeps?"

Kai, ignoring the pain in his head and leg bolted upright. "How did you know about the Jeeps? I never mentioned that part!"

Jack took a deep breath, pausing before offering a reply. "That's easy enough. We got the Jeeps, a couple of days before you started playing '*here fishy fishy*' with that shark. The ghosts in the lighthouse, the fog in the harbor, the corpse chase, the gold, all of it really happened. You haven't been dreaming, you've been remembering."

"You mean it's all true? You're tellin' me we're actually millionaires?"

"You got it dude. We're big time millionaires!"

St. Augustine, located along the coast of northeast Florida, is a popular vacation destination for folks from all over the country and from around the world. Established as a Spanish colony nearly four hundred and fifty years ago, it is the oldest city in America, older by several decades than the settlements of Plymouth and Jamestown.

While BAD LATITUDE is a work of fiction, the landmarks and locales described within the story actually exist, including *Rattlesnake Island*, making it possible for the reader to follow the adventure as part of a fun-filled visit to the Ancient City and the surrounding area. Just remember. The town is haunted, a favorite place for prowling ghost hunters, and the subject of many televised documentaries over the years. Don't believe it? Bring your camera and take a tour after dark, but make sure you're not alone when downloading your photos.

White sandy beaches, a desirable climate, art galleries, museums, outstanding accommodations and restaurants, quaint boutiques, unique attractions, nature and history, all great reasons to plan a stay in my hometown. Maybe you'll bump into Jack's Pop.

'Hang Loose'

You Can Also Visit - http://jaxpop.blogspot.com